SWAT TEAM SEVEN: OF THE CIRCLE

The Men of Five-0 #5

Dixie Lynn Dwyer

LOVEXTREME FOREVER

Siren Publishing, Inc.
www.SirenPublishing.com

A SIREN PUBLISHING BOOK
IMPRINT: LoveXtreme Forever

SWAT TEAM SEVEN: GODDESS OF THE CIRCLE
Copyright © 2013 by Dixie Lynn Dwyer

ISBN: 978-1-62740-444-0

First Printing: September 2013

Cover design by Les Byerley
All art and logo copyright © 2013 by Siren Publishing, Inc.

ALL RIGHTS RESERVED: This literary work may not be reproduced or transmitted in any form or by any means, including electronic or photographic reproduction, in whole or in part, without express written permission.

All characters and events in this book are fictitious. Any resemblance to actual persons living or dead is strictly coincidental.

Printed in the U.S.A.

PUBLISHER
Siren Publishing, Inc.
www.SirenPublishing.com

SWAT TEAM SEVEN: GODDESS OF THE CIRCLE

The Men of Five-0 #5

DIXIE LYNN DWYER
Copyright © 2013

Prologue

Kamea Mahalan held her breath. She could hear them rummaging through the house, making certain that there weren't any survivors. She lay hidden in the storage bench near her father's desk. She was barely small enough to fit into the compartment but she knew it was a life-or-death situation. Her father had taught her, since the day she could understand what danger was, how to find safety in there. While other kids worried about what outfit to wear to school, which dance classes they would take, Kamea practiced self-defense, became trained in survival techniques, and learned to trust no one but her mother, her father, and two brothers.

Now they were all dead. The sounds of their cries of pain were embedded in her mind. What sounded like growls, echoed in the distance and she couldn't even cover her ears. She tried to stop her mind from thinking. Any movement or sound would alert the intruders to her presence. Her entire family was dead. She just knew it. She practiced her breathing technique. Just as daddy had taught her to do in such a critical situation. She wasn't to move an inch, not try to run into the open where they could pick her off with a bullet, but instead lay silent as her family members screamed for mercy.

She heard the male voices, muffled by the thin layer of wood that pressed against her chest and face. Thank the lord that she wasn't claustrophobic. Her father told her that he had it made especially for her. He recently joked about coming up with a different plan and location because she was getting older.

Right above her, the chest opened. Her eyes widened in shock. Would they figure out the hidden space below? Would they capture her? Who were they? What did they look like? She wondered as her heart raced. Her throat felt as if she would choke for air and she prayed she didn't sneeze or make a sound. Kamea closed her eyes and held her breath.

"Why are you looking in there? She is dead, I told you. Didn't you see the body?" one asked.

"I am making sure. The neighbor's kid looked identical to the Mahalan child."

"We need to go. The job is done. Mahalan will no longer be a threat to the Morago organization or to Divanni and his cause. Let's go."

The Morago organization? Divanni?

She waited for what seemed like hours before she felt that it was safe to leave. What did the men mean by the neighbor's child? The thought hit her at once. Her best friend Cella was supposed to come over to play, but then the bad men came into the house.

As she slowly pushed the lid up, she absorbed the sight of the office, the quiet of the home, and the warm, tropical Hawaiian breeze that filtered through the curtains. Her heart pounded inside of her chest. She was twelve years old and as the tears rolled down her cheeks, she wondered, prayed, even though she knew in her gut that they weren't alive, that perhaps someone survived.

Kamea tiptoed out of the room. Her body shook with fear. Every small noise or creak made her jump. The light breeze pushed the shutters open a little further. As she looked, she noticed the torn curtains, the way the wooden shutters hung by broken hinges. The sounds were eerie to her ears.

She listened attentively for any indication that someone was still there but heard nothing. Her legs shook so terribly she thought her knees would give out. The moment she exited the hallway to the great room, she saw the blood splattered on the walls. She covered her mouth and gasped as what was left of her siblings' bodies came into view. She began to sob, looking through blurred vision at her mother next and then her father. As she heard a moan, she ran to his side, falling to her knees against the blood that oozed from his stomach. A gun remained in his hand. He looked at her. He appeared shocked and his eyes almost glowed with specks of dark green and yellow.

"Kamea?"

"Oh, Daddy, what should I do? Do I call for an ambulance?"

"No. Run away. Do as I taught you. Never return again. Never let anyone know you are alive. I love you."

He made an odd sound then remained staring at her as he took his last breath.

She sobbed as she reached down and took the gun that lay by his lifeless body. She checked the clip and knew that it was half-full. Kamea tried to just breathe and think about what her father taught her and the steps to take, but her mind was fuzzy and her body continued to shake. She closed her eyes, immediately envisioning him in her mind. He gave her directions. She could see him there, enforcing the importance of remembering the safety of the bench with the hidden compartment in his office and the duffle bag of items in the downstairs basement wall. She jumped up, taking in the horrific sight and feeling the urge to vomit. She couldn't leave evidence of her survival behind. Sooner than later, the ones responsible would find out that she was alive.

She ran to the basement door and down the stairs. Making her way into the hidden cubby in the back corner, she spotted the loose paneling and pulled it open. There sat the duffle bag. The one containing instructions about what she needed to do. This was really happening. She lost her entire family. She was completely alone.

Kamea pulled out the note. It was typed and orderly, just like her father. She read the three steps as she powered up the phone.

Hit #1 on speed dial. Use the five dollars to catch the bus a mile down the road. Take the hidden route and not the street.

Code words - Wolf Pack.

Kamea had no idea what that meant as she quickly gathered the bag and headed back upstairs. She thought she heard a noise as she snuck out the back door and into the tropical Hawaiian warmth. In the distance she heard the sound of vehicles as she quickly hurried through the thick trees and palms. She didn't want to take the chance of being caught. No one could be trusted. Only the person she contacted on the phone. She made it to the bus stop, heart pounding, palms sweating, and immediately boarded the bus and went to the far back. It was empty. She opened the phone and hit number one.

It rang multiple times and then a deep, yet calm voice answered.

"Kamea?"

"Password please," she responded with tears in her eyes and voice shaking.

"Wolf Pack."

She listened to the directions of the one on the phone then hung up. Closing her eyes, she waited for the trip to end and for what was to come.

"Melena. Melena."

Melena awoke in a cold sweat, sitting upright in bed. Her hand instinctively reached for the pistol under the pillow next to her in the king-sized bed.

She looked around her apartment and toward the blinds that blocked the sunlight and her view of the New York City skyline.

She heard Saxton's voice coming from the intercom on the side of the bed.

She reached for the button.

"I'm up. I'll be over in a bit."

Releasing the revolver, she rolled to the left and reached to the bedside table for the remote. For the last ten years, she woke up in the same way. A cold sweat, visions of her murdered family, and the smell of blood tainted her mind and her senses. Twenty-two years old and she was still frightened of the dark and whom or what potentially lurked in the shadows waiting to pounce on their prey. She would never be prey again. Vengeance was her life.

As she sat up, swinging her legs over the side of the bed, she pressed the button on the remote then tossed it back onto the table. Her head felt foggy. Every night for the last ten years, she dreamt of that dreadful day. The day she lost her entire family. Saxton and Tango, compatriots of her father, let her know from the start that they were her protectors and her guides through life. They were her trainers, her educators, her only connection to a relationship of some kind. She swallowed hard.

As she walked across the room to the bathroom, the blinds began to open and the gorgeous sunlight illuminated her dark bedroom.

After washing up, getting dressed and making a cup of coffee, she glanced at the manila folder on the table and then back out toward the New York City skyline. It was a gorgeous spring day. Last week, her travels brought her into the outskirts of Pennsylvania and a warehouse filled with antique furniture filled with illegal drugs. Coriano Morago was a modern-day crime boss who had his hands in everything from street drugs and stealing cars to working with terrorists. That had been how he got to her father and her family. Melena took a deep breath then felt the anger deep in her gut.

Her father worked for the US government. The Friday before that weekend that ended his life and the lives of his family members, he had engaged in a meeting with some wolves from an organization called the Brothers of Were. In that meeting he was acknowledged as having located the source of illegal arms and chemical weapons being exchanged for millions of dollars' worth of rare artifacts and jewels. Some dating back as far as during the Old Testament. But there was one particular treasure that had yet to be located and brought to the proper owners. It was a book of some kind. A book that gave names and locations of some sort of royalty to an organization she knew little about or cared to give respect to. Many people across a multitude of countries sought this collection of treasures and this book. Apparently the one who held the book and read from an inscription could unlock the information within. She wasn't sure if it was a fantasy story, but she knew that Morago and half the criminal element she came across were seeking this book out. None of that really mattered to her. Destroying Morago did.

She headed to the room to get dressed. She was going to work out and then do some recon on the next place of interest Morago owned. She uncovered the names of two known criminals that operated an illegal arms business on west Madison. It was an old warehouse, currently used to store new furniture for a major manufacturer. But in the back room there was a vault and in that vault were jewels from her family that Morago sold to these criminals. She wanted them back, and tonight, she would get them.

Chapter 1

"Are you sure about this?" Edric Dolberg asked Gideon, as he and their brothers, Chance, Mano, and Chordeo, prepared their weapons and looked over the blueprints of the building.

"I got word from headquarters that this operation has been identified, confirmed, and in need of removal," Gideon said.

Edric looked at his brother, the team leader of SWAT Team Seven. He was good at his job. He was hard core and thorough. He would never place the team, his pack brothers, in jeopardy.

"How come they want to take this operation out? There have been others that remain in operation, supplying the public with illegal drugs and weapons. So what's the deal with this one?" Chance asked.

Gideon looked at his brothers as he placed his weapon in his holster. To Edric, Gideon appeared angry and focused. His blue eyes looked more like black. He always got that way before a mission.

"The intelligence indicates these two men running the business have ties to terrorists. One of them has been identified as a member of an active terrorist cell. You know the drill. We don't allow such individuals the freedom to grow stronger. These men have the potential to cause some serious problems."

"Okay, Gideon. Just tell us what to look for. Is it a search-and-destroy mission or are we taking prisoners?" Chordeo asked.

Gideon glared at Chordeo then back toward the front of the vehicle and the direction the driver was going.

"We do what is necessary. My understanding is that we have backup on standby to take prisoners. However, the two assholes in charge need to be captured and escorted to the holding facility on the east side. If all goes well, we will personally be escorting those prisoners to the facility."

"Got it," Mano stated. Then the driver indicated that they were five minutes from the location.

* * * *

Melena felt entirely restricted in the black body suit she was wearing. But she couldn't risk getting her clothing snagged on some sharp edges or leaving her scent or her DNA behind. This was a not so easy job to pull off. Dashkin and Lunvolk ultimately worked for Count Lumanesque Divanni. That bastard thought the jewels of the wolf heritage belonged to a bunch of anti-American terrorists with no allegiance to anything but their greed and power. Well, tonight, they were going to lose some of those goodies, and perhaps her housemates and protectors, Saxton and Tango, were able to come through with notifying the authorities about precisely what these men were dealing in. Terrorism was not accepted or tolerated among legitimate were or humans.

Melena eased her way through the venting system. It was hot, it was a tight fit, and despite her large bust, she eased her way through to the main office where the vault was located.

As she crawled over the first section, she saw the many workers gathering up weapons and crates, labeling and doing whatever illegal criminal terrorists do with weapons as they distribute them. She hoped Saxton and Tango made the call. If so, these assholes would be locked up in no time. She just hoped the authorities didn't rush in to invade while she was still in the building. She needed to be quick. All her training, and of course extracurricular thrills, had to be worth the effort. She would succeed. She would find all the items and possessions that belonged to her family and she would one day be in possession of every one of them. Morago was an asshole.

Melena paused as she heard the muffled voices below. She was now over the makeshift conference room she'd discovered a few days ago in her first recon mission of the joint. *Son of a bitch, they're here tonight. Perfect.*

Melena felt her heart rate increase. This was so freaking dangerous. It thrilled her. Wasn't that sick? She had learned that revenge required commitment, determination, and obsession. She would get her revenge on Morago. She would.

Melena made her way to the next room, the office. The fact that Dashkin and Lunvolk were directly next door excited her. If all went well, they would be dead or behind bars tonight.

She quickly, but quietly opened the screen metal vent in the ceiling. She felt her chest tighten. *Maybe I shouldn't have had those three chocolate cookies today?*

She inhaled and squeezed her way through, grateful that the table was slightly to the right of the floor. She just made it as she quietly stepped down onto the table then floor. Swiftly, she secured the door, placed the chair under the knob as a precaution then turned toward the doorway that led to the vault.

Smiling wide she made her way to it and took a deep breath. She pulled the small bag from her waist and got her tools. In no time at all the door clicked and she was in.

"Holy shit."

There were so many sparkling items she thought it looked like a scene from some Indiana Jones movie. It was amazing and somehow as she scanned the area and her belly quivered with anticipation, she spotted the small wooden chest, her family heirloom, and still hopefully it contained some of the pendants and jewels of her ancestors.

She grabbed it and gave it a shake. It was heavy but she was determined.

Very easily she could take more right now, but that wasn't why she was here. The bricks of gold, the stacks of money were not earned but taken. It was drug money. This chest belonged to the Mahalan Family.

She climbed back up onto the table and placed the chest onto the shelf ceiling. Leaping upward, she swung her legs and got back up. She closed the screen metal grate and made her way slowly through the ventilation system. Right before she exited through the outdoor screen, she heard the commotion as the old, rusted, metal screen hit the ground. *Shit!*

They were there. The authorities were raiding the building. She needed to hurry.

* * * *

"On three!" Gideon called out then counted as they kicked open the side doorway.

Edric was taking up the rear when he heard what sounded like metal falling to the blacktop. He turned to the right and thought he saw something, but he couldn't investigate it now. Team Two would do it. They were human and local to the area.

As they made their way inside, there was little resistance. But then in a matter of seconds that all changed. The bullets began to fly toward them. Edric lowered to his knees, aimed, and fired a round of shots, taking down multiple men with firearms. Chance stuck to the side wall and shot down two other men who were heavily armed and firing shots at Chordeo. Edric watched as Gideon and Mano were jumped on by two big men. In a flash his brothers tossed the large men like rag dolls as more officers entered the building.

Task Force One, their cousins, joined them and helped to secure the area.

It was Edric, Gideon, and Mano who entered the offices in search of their two main suspects, Dashkin and Lunvolk. As bullets whizzed by their heads, Edric turned and fired, taking down two men in business suits.

Carefully they approached.

"They're still alive, Edric, but nice shots anyway," Mano teased him, and Edric shrugged his shoulders.

"They were going to kill you guys. I had no choice."

"And we appreciate that," Mano added, and they continued to secure the area.

* * * *

Gideon stood inside the surveillance room of the building and looked at the video surveillance. He was tipped off that something suspicious was going on as they entered a separate office and found a large vault, wide open. After backtracking to the sequence of events and the fact that a ventilation screen in the ceiling swung open while they were in there, they suspected something fishy was going on. Then Edric mentioned hearing a metal grate fall outside, right before they entered the building.

"What do you think, Gideon?" Van Fagan asked as they watched the video.

"He's slick and he knew what he was searching for," Gideon replied.

"Sure did, 'cause he entered and exited like a professional and he came here with a purpose. Not that I really give a shit since it was criminals who got ripped off," Van replied.

"That's no guy. That's a woman," Mano stated and Miele pushed him out of the way so he could take a better look.

"Fuck, he's right. Pause the tape right there. See, she's got curves," Miele stated.

"Interesting," Van replied.

"Let's scan to the outside of the building where Edric heard the metal grate fall. She obviously escaped through there," Gideon said with an attitude.

Sure enough they saw the woman escape through the side of the building then drop down like some cat woman three stories high. She landed perfectly and into a roll, while holding something in her arms.

"Impressive," Mano whispered.

"I wonder who she is and what exactly she took," Van stated.

"I guess we'll need to find out. Some of the items in there belong to families in were hierarchy."

"These men were into a lot of shit. They have a lot of money, too, so buying and collecting these items could just be a hobby," Mano said.

"Or, this woman in black could be connected to the robbery in the gala last weekend. A lot of items were stolen. Let's move. Van, you and your team look into the prints found at the scene. Our uncle is concerned that a similar hit may take place this weekend at the gala."

"We'll look into that, and Dani has some pull on the streets. Maybe we can get an identity on the mysterious woman in black," Van replied, and they chuckled. Gideon, however, didn't like the direction this was going in. It seemed to him that the city was running amuck. Weres were going rogue, people weren't following the were laws and looking to prosper illegally. The last few cases they showed up on didn't go well at all. Something strange was going on.

Chapter 2

Melena awoke with a start again. Same thing every night. It was a wonder how she even functioned during the day, yet it seemed that her body could survive on very little sleep. She wondered when that would catch up with her. Last night had been a bit scary. She didn't want to get caught, but she did stick around to see the huge were SWAT team make their way into the building. The word on the streets was that Dashkin and Lunvolk survived. They weren't taken out. Too bad. She wouldn't have given their death a second thought. She also heard that the items in the vault were transferred to a holding facility at one of the local precincts. Thank God she had gotten her items when she did or she may have lost the opportunity forever.

As she looked at another folder, sitting on the table by the window, she wondered if she would ever really be free. Could she ever lead a normal life, even after she destroyed and killed Coriano Morago?

Melena investigated the reasoning behind Morago killing her father and family. Although Saxton tried his hardest to keep her at bay, she pushed. She learned that Morago nearly lost everything as Melena's father exposed Morago's plan. The Brothers of Were killed over a dozen of Morago's men. Morago got away with the jewels and members of the Brothers of Were exposed the terrorists. The book remained missing and knowledge of the existence of supernatural beings was exposed to her. Men who could shift into wolves, vampires, fairies, healers, and magic of all kinds actually existed. That had taken some time to get used to.

Melena was still trying to get over the fact that were packs existed, and Saxton and Tango could shift from human to wolf in seconds. It had come as an even greater shock to learn that her family had were blood running through the bloodline.

If I were a wolf, I would rip Morago's throat out.

Melena could feel the burn of hatred practically in her throat as she stared out at the city. She missed Hawaii, even though she was only a child when she was forced to leave. She missed learning about her Polynesian family history and what could possibly be hidden within the family genes. Whenever she tried to remember her childhood and the life she had in Hawaii, she couldn't. It was as if her mind blocked out the memories. More than likely it was a coping mechanism brought on by the trauma of her family's massacre. A therapist would have a field day with her.

She knew she was a lot like her father, Zeikele. Saxton often reminded her of that fact when she stubbornly rejected his direct order. Once or twice, Saxton or Tango had referred to her father as Sir Mahalan, but that stopped very quickly.

Melena chuckled to herself. Saxton and Tango were excellent trainers and powerfully strong men. During her training, she learned to not only fight against men more powerful and stronger than her physically, but also against weres. Although, supposedly there were more good weres working for the government than against it. All she knew was that whenever she was in the heat of a fight she sensed a change within her. It was just beneath the surface but seemed unobtainable.

Melena sighed. Saxton and Tango were going to be pretty pissed off about her sneaking into the facility last night and taking her family's heirloom chest without their assistance. She'd needed to do that. She'd needed to show them that she was more than capable of handling things on her own. She had yet to go through the things inside the chest, but she knew she needed to get them out of there. Something was pulling her to take the chance and break into the building. She couldn't explain what it was, but it was strong. Besides, no one but a Mahalan had the right to possess such treasures.

She didn't trust people or weres. She was after one thing and one thing only. Melena would not rest until Coriano Morago was dead and his entire organization destroyed. If she could take out the count, then the world would be a better place.

She clicked on the remote to the television and watched one of the local news channels. She immediately saw the words "special report" glowing in red at the bottom of the screen. The reporter was standing in front of a building, there was a lot of smoke, and the sound of gunfire echoed in the distance. The reporter looked scared.

"I'm standing about fifty yards from the scene now. You can hear the exchange of gunfire between police and a group of gang members. One of the officers I grabbed on the way over here explained that there was a drug bust in process that went wrong. The fire raging behind me that continues to burn cannot be extinguished. The gang members started the blaze in an attempt to destroy evidence. It is believed, but not confirmed, that this factory was a cover for cocaine production and other drugs and may be connected to last night's SWAT team raid. Millions of dollars in gold and antiques were found in the building along with large stacks of money. That has not been confirmed. Right now, I have confirmation that seven officers have been seriously injured and multiple others killed."

Before the reporter could continue, another explosion rocked the building and the reporter fell to the ground, the camera man must have fallen, too, because the picture showed an upside down version of the ground and then went back to the main studio.

Melena turned off the television. This was exactly why she wanted Morago and the others taken down. She just couldn't figure out why the circle of elders, who represented all weres, wouldn't issue the command.

Ten years of being alone, of dealing with hearing her family being brutally murdered, provided her strength and determination to succeed. She excelled in school and landed the government job, working for one of the higher-ups in the city council. It didn't take long to figure out that the city council was merely a front for a secret program run by Fagan wolf pack members and supposedly a vampire. She never saw the vamp, but heard he was quite the looker and very powerful. That wasn't her interest in being part of the organization. It was a means to finding out more about Coriano Morago and his associates so she could take them down. The government should eliminate people like Coriano Morago. Instead they continued to allow his freedom and his illegal activities to continue. He killed one of their own. So why was he allowed to live?

She didn't have much respect for authority and she sure as shit wouldn't listen to any were officials, despite Saxton and Tango's explanation of how were authority worked. She wasn't able to shift into the ferocious beast so their rules didn't apply to her.

She heard the knock on the door and headed over to answer it. She knew it was Tango or Saxton.

"Good morning, sunshine. Late night again?" Tango asked as he walked into her apartment.

The building was basically empty and sat on the corner of an old business district street, twenty minutes from Manhattan.

"I was working on the project and hoping to add the fifth member. It's been crazy."

"I bet. Are you going to work out today or skip it because you're too tired?" She shook her head at his teasing. Tango was six feet tall, with lots of muscles but very lean. His abs of steel were impressive, and as she processed through puberty, she couldn't help but have a sort of crush on him and Saxton. Saxton was a big, burly man of steel. He was the serious one while Tango was the jokester.

"You know that I'm going to work out. Quit it."

"I can't help but tease my little human."

"Oh nice. I appreciate that, wolf man."

"Wolf man?" he asked then chuckled.

"Did you get a look at the file?"

"I was going to look again this morning. I suppose Saxton is waiting on me to go over everything in detail?"

"He sure is. So whenever you're ready, meet us downstairs. Oh, and perhaps you'd like to explain why you snuck out last night to do that job on your own?"

"Oh, I don't know, maybe so that you two can stop treating me like a child."

He looked at her sideways.

"Be ready to explain and bring along whatever it is you decided to take. You're lucky you didn't get caught. All that stuff is drug money, honey. You have plenty of your own money."

"I didn't take money."

He raised his hand.

"I'll wait until you come downstairs. That way you don't have to repeat your story twice."

She smiled as he left the apartment. She closed the door then walked back over toward the windows. Things were becoming monotonous. She yearned for some change, some excitement and perhaps a bit of revenge on a small scale until she could truly seek the ultimate revenge on Morago. She felt antsy.

She knew that she needed to be cautious. Even with the city council. But the ones in charge at the city council sniffed her, investigated her, and still gave her the job despite seeming more human than anything else. Her assets had a lot to do with getting hired, too. She was built well and that was what ultimately mattered in the position as liaison for her boss, Xavier Dolberg. He was a newly appointed member to a brand-new program she helped to develop.

Xavier kept her under wraps. Her identity was well hidden and most correspondence took place through phone and Internet. But tonight would be the first night she would be somewhat exposed. Melena already asked Xavier not to divulge her position of liaison, but instead have her act as more of a company representative. That would give her the opportunity to still support Xavier and the city council's agenda, but secretly, she could also achieve her own agenda. Count Lumanesque Divanni was attending this evening and hopefully someone from the Filletto organization as well as Morago's.

What she still didn't understand was how the government seemed to operate. There were continuous stories on the news about murders, vicious crimes, and acts of violence. Who had the final say in determining who lived and who died, who was punished and who was allowed their continued freedom?

Her father was a higher-up in the military and the government. How could they dismiss his death and the death of his family so easily? Did these were mean more than humans?

The circle of elders was not in charge of her. They were nothing to her because she meant nothing to them, nor did her father. Where were they when she was twelve years old and all alone? How come they didn't help Saxton and Tango? Not that her two wolves needed help. They meant everything to her. But she couldn't forget her father. His sacrifice had not placed any of these modern-day criminals behind bars or six feet under. Well, she would.

Her anger grew stronger as she finished her coffee and rose from the table. She needed to work out, shower, then prepare for tonight's event. She was kind of looking forward to a more formal affair and getting to know the players in this little were organization. This was the beginning of her revenge.

* * * *

"Explain," Saxton stated, with his arms crossed in front of his chest. He was so worried about Melena last night, but he knew that she was going to go in there. He was completely impressed with the fact that no one had detected her until the surveillance videos showed a person in black. The investigators were asking questions, but he had people to help pull attention away from her. She wouldn't get identified either way. Now he wondered if the magic spell over her had something to do with this job she did.

Instead of allowing him and Tango to make the plans, she decided to call him a few minutes before she entered the building to tell him what she was doing and of course it was too late to get there to help her.

"You know those things belonged to my family, to me. I was just taking them back." She leaned against the wall.

"And if you were caught?"

"You or Tango would have paid my bail and got me out of there."

"No, you would have been prosecuted and charged," Tango added.

"No, not when all those repeat offenders keep getting let off the hook. It would have been a slap on the wrist."

"You shouldn't have gone."

"I wanted to. I did it and I wasn't caught."

"You were seen on video camera."

She squinted her eyes at him as if she didn't believe his statement. She looked so cute. She was a mature woman and soon her fate would step in and change her life.

"Hence, the very black outfit and mask."

"Either way, we now are trying to get the detectives to ignore that footage and focus on the fact that they captured Dashkin and Lunvolk," Saxton said.

"They should be charging those two with everything, especially after the other raid and all those innocent people being shot and killed," Tango stated.

"Exactly."

Saxton stared at Melena. There would be no use in arguing with her. Now he wondered if the chest contained the brooch.

"So, what was in the chest?" he asked as he unfolded his arms and took a seat behind the desk.

"I haven't looked inside of it yet." She lowered her eyes. He knew this would be tough for her. Anything having to do with her family, remembering them and her past, brought on sadness and also made Melena close up her emotions.

"Want us to look inside of it with you?" Saxton suggested.

She looked up, appearing surprised at his suggestion but then she smiled and nodded her head.

"Okay, go get the box."

He was surprised as she opened the door, reached down, and pulled a black duffle bag into the room. She walked over to his desk and pulled out the plain, brown chest.

She ran her fingers gently over the wood and traced the letter *M*, with her finger.

"I don't have anything of my mother's or father's. I hope this contains something important." She opened it up. He identified the magnificent brooch immediately as Melena reached for a locket, some rings and earrings, and then caressed the diamonds that lined the upper part of the inside of the box.

"That brooch, Melena, is so very important to your family and to the were world," Saxton whispered as she picked it up and looked at the multitude of pearls, diamonds, and floral gold leaves.

"This right here?"

He nodded his head as she stared at it, held it in both hands, then smiled wide.

"It is important. I sensed it immediately, Saxton. What is it and what does it mean?"

"When the gods decide the time is right, they will tell you, Melena, but for now, we must keep it in safekeeping. It is yours and no one else should ever possess it," Saxton said as apprehension filled his heart. He would do whatever was necessary to keep Melena safe and alive.

* * * *

"Well, I'd say that someone wants our attention taken away from the woman in black," Xavier Dolberg stated to his nephew Gideon over the phone.

"Why is that?" Gideon asked.

"Beats the hell out of me, but it is coming from higher up. Perhaps she was working for the good guys? I did receive some intel that someone tipped your Commander and headquarters off on the building and its occupants. You did receive the call to move in without a lot of notice?"

"That is correct. We got the call and we moved in very quickly."

"Well it worked out. Dashkin and Lunvolk are done. Plus, they seemed to be behind the warehouse fire and the situation from the other night as well."

"We're still trying to get over that mess. We lost good men and innocent civilians. All over drugs and guns. What a waste."

"I know, Gideon. The council is under a lot of pressure right now. Some revamping is necessary and protocol doesn't allow for much leeway."

"Bullshit. Just eliminate the scum and secure the good guys. It's a no-brainer as far as I'm concerned."

Xavier chuckled. Gideon and his brothers were fierce and straight to the point. They didn't care for fluff or bureaucracy.

"How about the vault? Were you able to confiscate and find what it was you were searching for, Uncle?" Gideon asked, and Xavier felt his chest tighten. He was extremely disappointed.

"No. It wasn't there. Our intel was incorrect."

"Perhaps the woman in black, whom we are no longer allowed to pursue, had something to do with it?" Gideon asked, and Xavier suddenly felt on edge.

"Maybe, under the radar of course, you and your brothers could try and find out?"

"I'm on it. Later."

Gideon hung up and Xavier leaned back in his chair and sighed. He needed to secure the circle and get this Security Ring up and running. Perhaps Morago and his associates didn't locate and take the item as he had thought. If they did possess it and then located that book, the circle would be vulnerable to destruction.

* * * *

A few days had passed and both Saxton and Tango expressed concern over her identity being compromised. She probably shouldn't have also broken into Morago's warehouse days prior to breaking into Dashkin and Lunvolk's. But those were two different circumstances.

She'd secured her family's important brooch, whatever that was all about, and she broke into the Morago's warehouses and found some interesting files on his office computer in regards to illegal activities. It seemed to her that Morago was planning something big. Something that would ensure a position in some kind of group.

The country seemed to be running amuck lately, with the news media broadcasting certain stories while bypassing others. Interesting enough, it seemed through her position in the city council as liaison to Xavier Dolberg that werewolves controlled everything. They ran the government, the law enforcement, and most other forms of public and private organizations people had to report to. The fact that most humans had no idea how surrounded by werewolves they were at all times kind of pissed Melena off. But every time she felt anger or upset over those who ruled, something in her reminded Melena of her job. She didn't want anyone else to experience the loss and danger that she had. Being in charge of the new project with the city council was huge.

She looked over the documents and notes she had written on her findings at Morago's warehouse. The letters TAMW were the title of different files that were encoded. There was also a logo from some pharmaceutical company or lab called United Shield. Saxton was working on finding more information. The one thing she did take with her from the office was a set of silver knives under glass. They were different sizes, the smallest being a switchblade. She would bring that with her tonight. Melena wasn't sure why she took them, but the largest reminded her of one her father once carried with him.

Melena was in shape, well trained by two members of an elite organization the government denied existed. Saxton and Tango held allegiance to her father for things that they wouldn't divulge but obviously meant the world to them. They took her under their care immediately ten years ago and ultimately trained her.

More often than not, they acted like her fathers, and that was a bit annoying.

They had argued for years about her desire for revenge. She nearly attempted to escape and seek that revenge before she was ready as she allowed anger and pure hatred to rule her mind. Tango had stopped her right before she exposed herself to Coriano. If he hadn't been there, there was no doubt that she would have been killed.

She was smarter now. She was older, twenty-two, in amazing shape and trained in the use of everything from explosives to firearms. She was her own arsenal and wouldn't need a soul to help her accomplish her goal. The last ten years were spent in preparation of taking down Coriano Morago and securing a position in the city council. Coriano Morago wouldn't know what hit him. She would destroy him slowly, making his life miserable and his fat wallet empty. Revenge was a powerful weapon and so was patience.

Chapter 3

Gideon Dolberg sighed in annoyance as he spoke with Julius Kordosky, a vampire and associate. The man had such a powerful attitude and way about him. It wasn't that Julius was pompous, but he was determined and assertive. As members of The Secret Order of the Brothers of Were, Gideon and his four brothers, Mano, Chordeo, Chance, and Edric, all held allegiance to the circle and to were law. For years they had searched for a means to secure the circle and its members, but it seemed that society and greed had influenced some of the members and now it was their job to help weed those individuals out.

"I get why you decided to pretend interest in the illegal activity, Julius. However, catching Count Divanni and Filletto must be done in a certain fashion. Besides, as we both know, there is someone who is keeping those two wolves protected from arrest and prosecution for their crimes. We need to be careful."

"Gideon, I called you because of the bit of information I overheard. There is a secret society that could possibly hold those individuals that are plaguing your circle of laws. I would like nothing more than to destroy these greedy, disloyal wolves just as you want to. It's just a hunch, but the urge to inform you was great. You know how I am about instincts and signs. The magic of the gods works in mysterious ways."

Gideon snorted. His life had done a complete change ten years ago when he and his brothers realized that the mate they never had the chance to physically meet had died. When a wolf's mate dies, a part of the wolf does. He and his brothers had quite the reputation as nasty, hard-core enforcers. They did things under their legal right but also with gusto and forcefulness that would send fear to anyone with any bit of common sense.

"You don't have to tell me about magic or the gods' surprise intentions. I will have Mano look into this society. Do you have a name?"

"Unfortunately I don't. However, there is this warehouse that Filletto and Morago have set up for business. I believe that location was mentioned."

"I appreciate the heads-up. Will we see you tonight at the gala?"

"Perhaps. I was stiffed out of a delivery of very rare jewels."

"Don't say any more. I do not want to be held in contempt with having knowledge of your extracurricular activities to get information to bring down these men."

Julius chuckled.

"Good-bye, friend."

Gideon disconnected the call and sighed. As he walked over toward the mirror and fixed the bow tie on his tux, he took in the sight.

He was a very large man and an even larger wolf. His jet-black hair was wavy and past his shoulders and he didn't feel like pulling it back for this event. He was a wolf, a soldier, and an enforcer. This was his life and the lives of his four brothers. There was never going to be anything more.

The words brought on instant thoughts of his mate and his brothers. That day would stand out in his mind forever. Although they were young, only a hundred years of age, every wolf longed to find their mate and to feel complete. They had not truly been searching for her because they knew that finding a mate was rare. Especially considering their dedication and commitment as Brothers of Were enforcers. They were asked to be part of the elite group and because their mate was dead, they were available at the drop of a hat.

He remembered walking into the massacre of bodies and sensing her there. He could smell her hidden amongst the mix of her family's blood. Her body more than likely shredded like her siblings. Gideon closed his eyes and felt his chest tighten. She was dead, before he had the opportunity to see her, to know her, never mind possess her. Even if she had survived, he and his brothers would have had to wait at least eight to ten years for her to mature into a woman. But during that time they would have protected her, guided her in decisions and ultimately won her heart before any other wolf could stake a claim.

Gideon's heart ached and he clenched his fists by his side and stared at his reflection in the mirror. She was gone. There was nothing he and his brothers could do about it. Fighting for the circle, protecting were law, and destroying those out to hurt the circle and its members was their lives now.

He cleared his mind and puffed out his chest. He was itching for a fight and maybe he'd get his wish and take out some of the pent-up anger now flowing through his veins. That's when he felt the slight tingling in his belly. He took pause and tried to identify the emotion.

Something was up. Something was going to happen soon. What? He wasn't certain, but the gods were.

* * * *

"I really hope this is not just another fucking waste of time. I mean, we've been to these damn galas and protect these members of the circle and for what? The majority of people there are oblivious," Edric Dolberg stated as he leaned back on the sofa. He had worked out, showered, and now waited for the clock to reach six and for Gideon to give the order that it was time to head out.

"I hear ya, Edric. Believe me, I hate wearing fucking tuxedoes just like the rest of you, but this is part of our job responsibilities and besides, Uncle Xavier asked us to attend as undercover security. If we're not working in SWAT Team Seven, then we're working for the

Secret Order or being subcontracted out by Sam or Ava. We're good at what we do. This is a piece of cake compared to some of our other missions," Chance said then winked, acting like his overconfident and pompous self. His brother was slick and oh, so very charming when it came to the ladies.

"First of all, look at the size of us. Anyone with a fucking brain could see we're not regular guys. Throw in the tight fucking tuxedo and shit, my wolf is annoyed and angry. I prefer to be knocking people around, letting them meet my fists or better yet, tearing some throats out."

"Well you're just going to have to deal with it. More than likely your wolf is still not calmed down after that raid in the warehouse and the fact that the woman in black got away. Throw in the stint in Ireland prior to that. We were in were form a lot and got to enjoy the O'Brian land and all its natural beauty. Plus, there's still that issue with Warnerbe Pierce, claiming that we weren't protecting him last week at the event."

"That asshole had it coming. He fucks women as often as he changes his underwear. He was bound to get caught by the bimbo he was dating steadily. It's more than that. Things have been kind of quiet around here, haven't they?" Edric asked then took a slug of beer from the beer can.

"Ah hell, Edric, why did you just jinx the evening? I've got plans with a certain brunette if all goes well," Mano said as he joined them in the living room.

He reached into the bowl of pretzels and grabbed a handful.

"What's going on, Edric?" Chance asked him and Edric sighed.

"I don't know. I just have this odd feeling. It's been with me for the last few days now."

"You haven't felt right since that botched drug bust we were called to after the mess by the local authorities," Mano said.

Edric thought about that a minute. It sucked to pull up onto the scene thinking they were going to aid in arrests but instead an all-out blood bath lay before them. Innocent lives were destroyed and children left without parents. He thought about their mate and her family. The way they were killed and left shredded up made him have a hollow heart.

"It was a massacre," Edric said.

"It was a fucking mess but the circumstances were out of our control. Our team would have handled it differently," Mano stated.

"Our team wouldn't have gone in there gung ho like those guys did. The men responsible wouldn't be walking or breathing right now."

"It doesn't matter. Chance. It was over before we got there. I just felt bad for those families. I still don't understand why the circle didn't eliminate the gang responsible," Edric said with disgust.

"Because there is more to what happened than we were told." Gideon, their Alpha, appeared with their brother Chordeo accompanying him. Gideon was fixing his bow tie and straining his neck as if the monkey suit was too tight. That was how they would all feel shortly when they, too, had to get dressed.

"Well we figured it had to be tied to someone of importance," Chance added.

"It is more than that, brothers. Chordeo and I have been in contact with the Valdamar Pack members. They understand our upset, but indicated that there was more at stake here and that the Filletto organization could not be penalized at this time," Gideon explained.

"That sounds like a bunch of red tape to me," Edric replied.

"More like a load of bullshit. Let's face it, we have no say in these matters. Look how the call came up to drop the investigation on the chick in black from Dashkin's warehouse. I'd like to know who she is and what she was doing there," Mano said.

"We get our orders and we do our jobs. Let's get ready," Chordeo stated firmly then turned around and left the room.

He was right. Even though each of them were part of SWAT Team Seven and the Secret Order and were highly trained Alpha wolves, they were servants to the circle of elders. That would never change. So why was Edric feeling so negative about their responsibilities tonight?

* * * *

Melena dressed in a stylish red fitted dress. Saxton thought it was sad that Melena couldn't go by Kamea, her Polynesian name. So often, her family name, 'Kamea', would nearly slip off his tongue. He wondered if he were getting soft. Melena had that effect on him, especially since he practically raised her with Tango.

She was strapping on the second heel as she stepped onto the high bench. Saxton stood in the doorway watching her. She was so beautiful. Although he was way older and a wolf, he found her incredibly sexy and attractive. He worried about her and the men who might try to seduce her. The thought brought on emotions he wasn't quite able to identify. It wasn't jealousy. It was true concern. A woman of Polynesian descent, she would surely stand out in a crowd. Her long wavy brown hair was now covered with a blonde wig. She still looked amazing.

She had the face of a glamorous movie star, bold light green eyes, enhanced by her tan complexion and lips, plump, seductive and ripe. She admitted to him once, that she thought about kissing him. He explained that it was natural for her to feel a bond with him and Tango, because they were the only two male figures in her life with no relation to her family blood line. After that moment, he had thought about kissing her, tasting her and taking away the pain that continued to give her sleepless nights. But he couldn't. Her father, their closest friend had left them with the responsibility to take care of Melena if anything ever happened to him. He prayed that the magic spell surrounding her and her identity remained intact.

Saxton heard Tango approaching and one look at him as Tango glanced into the room and he paused to look at Melena.

"She is stunning. I hope she can handle this."

Saxton stepped further into the room.

"I can see the switchblade, Melena."

She turned toward him, placing her hands on her hips, with her leg still upright on the bench and the dress way up her gorgeous thigh.

"I know that, Saxton. I'm not planning on being in this position when I'm at the party. I'll be all classy and conservative. Don't you worry. I'm just glad I convinced Xavier to let me wear the wig and remain somewhat disguised. He didn't seem too happy about it. I expected him to ask questions but he didn't." She adjusted the garter belt that held the silver switchblade. She stepped down as he and Tango approached. Xavier didn't ask, because the magic spell over Melena was that strong.

"Conservative and that dress do not go hand in hand, Melena. Couldn't you find something less provocative?" Tango asked, and she smiled then gave them both hugs.

"No worries. From our investigations over the past couple of years, Count Lumanesque Divanni likes women who are fashionable."

Melena pressed her chest out.

"Christ, Melena, you're…"

"Well endowed," she replied to Tango as she pressed the palms of her hands along her breasts to her narrow waist and winked.

"They look good, don't they? I mean, I think I'm a fully grown woman," she added as she turned side to side in front of the mirror.

Tango ran his hands through his hair and turned away from her.

Saxton crossed his arms in front of his chest and stared at her as she looked to Tango's back then back toward Saxton.

"Watch your sassiness. Remember the game plan. This is only recon you're doing. We're allowing this because you've been working for Xavier for years now. Your goal of intensifying the protection for circle members has taken precedence over everything else. You should try to converse with Donovan Kylton while you are there. If you decide to choose him as a member for the new Security Ring, then he may have to step down as a member of the circle. Remember, this is not about revenge."

"I wouldn't quite say that. I still seek my revenge. You both have taught me patience. But mark my words, Morago will die."

"Melena." Saxton gave her a stern expression, like that a father gave his child.

"Revenge was not what your father wanted," Tango added, turning toward Melena.

"Oh, are we at this again. Blah, blah, blah, I am a woman with a mysterious past. My identity must remain a secret. For what? The two of you have kept so many secrets about my true identity away from me. 'With time,' you say. Well how frustrating is that? I want to know. I want to be prepared. Will Morago come after me if he knows I am the child of Zeikele Mahalan? Let him come. Let him find out that he was not successful in eliminating the threat." She threw her hands up into the air as she walked toward the bed and grabbed her small black clutch.

"Please, Melena. We are working toward destroying Filletto, Divanni, and Morago from within. We must be careful. Besides, securing the circle of elders and getting rid of the bad members is necessary. "

"Saxton is right, Melena. There will be other wolves there and certainly both human and male wolves who will try to…engage you with their charms."

"Oh brother. I'm twenty-two and do not need to have the whole sex conversation with you two. Besides, I've been doing recon for the past three years with Xavier's organization."

"Melena, you're an innocent," Saxton began to say when Melena placed her hand on his shoulder then stood up on tiptoes to kiss his cheek.

She whispered into his ear. "How do you know I am?" Then she started to head toward the door but he grabbed her wrist and stopped her.

"Tango and I make it our business to know everything. Including your little obsession with romance books."

"So what? I like romance novels. What's the big deal?"

"Not just romance novels, but erotic romance novels," Tango said. Saxton saw her cheeks redden as she lowered her eyes.

"Just be careful, Melena. Wolves like to share their women and we'd hate to see you taken advantage of like that, because you believe what you read," Saxton added.

She suddenly became very serious.

"I know what I'm doing and I know how my life must be. You two are all I have. You are both wolves and neither of you have ever made a move on me. I get it. I'm destined for loneliness."

"Melena!" Saxton gave her a stern expression. He looked down into her gorgeous green eyes and remembered her youth, the fearful child who witnessed her family being massacred. She somehow pulled off an escape and contacted them as her father had taught her. He would never forget that day and nor would Tango.

"You are the most stunning woman and amazing person we have ever met. Wolves look to settle with their mate. We have cared for you and provided for you, but there will come a time when your mate will find you. He will be very lucky to have you. Be smart, Melena. Remember all we have taught you about humans and about weres. Your life, your entire existence depends upon it."

She smiled at him then glanced at Tango who stood right next to them.

"You both are more than just friends, you are my family, and I love you both. Now how about we go take care of some business?"

They headed out of the bedroom. But despite Saxton's words to Melena, he still had a heavy heart and some reservations about tonight's gala.

Chapter 4

"It's crowded. I don't like crowds," Chordeo said to his brothers through his wrist mic. He pulled on his collar trying to release the tightness, for the umpteenth time.

"None of us do. Just focus on the orchestra playing the music. You like that classical shit," Mano said, and Chordeo could see him from where he stood by the upper balcony. There were a lot of people at the event and a lot of pack members of importance.

"I'm bored," Chordeo said.

"*Remain on alert. There are a lot of different people here and I don't think the antiques are the only point of interest,*" Gideon said through their mind link this time as he smiled and nodded at some group of men admiring a collection of jewelry.

"*I found my point of interest. Look at the blonde in the red dress speaking with Divanni. I've never seen her before,*" Chance stated. Chordeo was the closest as he eyed the beauty. She was definitely stunning and immediately caught the attention of many men. In a matter of seconds, she was surrounded by not just one wolf of importance, but seven. Four of which Chordeo personally didn't care for.

"*Son of a bitch, who is she?*" Chance asked as he began to make his way closer toward Chordeo and the woman.

"*Remain focused. I do not know whom you four are watching but you are supposed to be securing the area for the elders. Focus!*" Gideon raised his voice.

Chordeo continued to watch the woman. Despite being the only female surrounded by seven men, it seemed she felt quite at ease. In fact, she was holding on to Divanni's arm as he introduced her to Warnerbe Pierce, a member of the circle of elders and a pain in the ass.

Chordeo listened in on the conversation as he kept a close eye on the blonde. Her hair was short. Way shorter than he liked on his women but its style was appealing. Her hair accentuated her face and her long, tan neck. From where he stood he could tell she had large breasts under the tight bodice of her dress. This woman had class and sophistication. Who was she?

"I do not know the name. You say the last name is Zekar?" Count Divanni asked the blonde.

"Yes, sir, Melena Zekar. I'm afraid that I'm not really anyone of importance. I assist the city council with parties like this one. Not spectacular, like a countess, I'm afraid."

"Ah, my dear, your beauty alone is quite intriguing. You've gained my interest."

Chordeo rolled his eyes. How lame of a line was that? Then suddenly Chordeo felt his hackles rise. A man, dressed in a black cape over his black tuxedo descended the stairs directly next to where the small group of men conversed with the woman. As she stepped to the side, he caught a whiff of her scent while simultaneously acknowledging the presence of the vampire.

"Remain calm, Chordeo. It's Julius," Gideon stated through the mic.

"*Something is up, Gideon. Her scent is amazing. Despite the fact that she is wearing a lot of perfume, it's pulling at my wolf.*"

"*What?*" Chance and Mano asked at the same time.

Chordeo moved closer.

"*Hold back, brother. I'll be there momentarily,*" Gideon added.

Chordeo listened to the vampire speak. But his thoughts and his focus were on the blonde. He stared at her body and felt his cock harden. *What the fuck?*

"I thought you would be here, wolf. We have some business to discuss and it cannot wait," Julius said.

"There's no need to be so abrupt. After all, there is a beautiful woman present," Divanni said, and the vampire looked at the blonde. Again Chordeo's hackles rose. It was taking everything he had to not grab the woman and inhale her scent while protecting her from the eyes and the power of wolves and the vampire. He didn't know what was coming over him but he knew he felt possessive.

The vampire stared into the eyes of the woman. He held her gaze, his eyes widened, and then he gave a small smirk. "You, I will surely like to get to know better."

"Am I too late to join this little gathering?"

Chordeo saw the man enter the group and Divanni stared at him in anger. The blonde slowly back stepped out of there and so did Warnerbe Pierce.

"Who is the man in the white tux?" Chordeo asked his brothers.

"That is one of Filletto's main guys. I'm right around the corner. I have you all in my sights," Gideon said.

A group of men approached from the left. The man in the white tux smirked. "You didn't think he would find out about the exchange, Divanni?" the man in the white tux asked.

"I don't know what you're talking about. This is not the time or the place. If you'll excuse me," Divanni began to say and move toward the blonde, taking her hand as if he were escorting her away from the scene.

"Not so fast, Count. Morago wants to know where the jewels are." The man in the white tux bared his teeth, and a low growl filled the area. The group of men surrounded the count and the blonde. As one of them reached to take hold of her arm, she reversed the move on him then shoved him into the center of the men. She began to exit down the staircase and Divanni followed. In a flash the men began to go after the other men as the vampire tossed those who dared to challenge him. Julius strained his neck to watch and see where the blonde went. None of this sat right with Chordeo.

"*Stay out of it. Something is going on here. Let Julius handle this situation. I'll explain later. Mano, Chance, do you have Donovan in your sights?*" Gideon asked as he and Chordeo exited the area and followed Divanni.

"*The item is secured.*" Chance replied.

"*Oh my lord, who is that?*" Chance asked over the mic.

"*Who?*" Chordeo asked.

"*I've got the blonde bombshell in my sights along with the count. They are three, two, one step from me. Fuck,*" Chance said.

Chordeo glanced at Gideon who heard Chance raise his voice through their mind link. They were at the bottom of the stairs. Chance was following the blonde and the count. The two people were talking to Donovan Kylton.

Chordeo and Gideon came upon Chance.

"What's wrong?"

"I know what you meant, brother, when you said there was something about her scent. It's glossed over with perfume. She's wearing a ton of it. But I swear, my wolf is on alert. So are certain body parts," Chance said as the men and Filletto's guy ascended the stairs and approached their group. Before the Dolberg Pack could move, a fight broke out.

* * * *

Melena was enjoying the party and she found the vampire to be quite attractive. But when he looked at her, she felt the sensation of comfort and immediately remembered what Saxton had told her about vampires and their powers. She blocked him immediately, which made him smirk. She hoped that she hadn't projected any information about herself to him. Saxton and Tango warned her about mind influence. But something tingled inside as he eyed her over. She also felt as if she knew him or he was familiar. However, she never met a vampire and recently the only vampire she was researching was one named Julius Kordosky. Could this vampire be Julius? Was she attracted to him? Now wouldn't that be interesting to lose her virginity to a vampire? She chuckled at the thought and then hoped that she hadn't projected those thoughts to the vampire, who immediately smiled and showed interest. *Shit.* That wouldn't be good. She needed to remain focused here.

Where was Xavier anyway? She glanced around, hardly listening to Divanni speaking with Donovan Kylton when she sensed someone else's eyes upon her. Goose bumps covered her skin and awareness encompassed her being. She searched for the culprit. A quick glance to the right and there stood some huge-ass guy in a tux. He appeared too uncomfortable for the tuxedo and on guard. That was when she figured he had to be security for someone. They made eye contact and she swallowed hard. He was quite the bit of eye candy, too. Her belly quivered and her nipples hardened. She had to remind herself that this party was not for her pleasure but a means to an end to Morago. *There must be something wrong with me. The first few good-looking men and I'm ready to spread my thighs and give up my virginity to strange wolves or even a vampire. Yikes!*

As the situation turned a bit unsteady, she decided to leave before jeopardizing her identity and purpose here. She could hear some commotion going on behind her. When suddenly, Count Lumanesque Divanni grabbed her hand and escorted her away from the scene. As an escape method, she wasn't complaining. He, too, was charming and good looking. Besides the fact that he was a count, he seemed nice. She knew from the investigations Tango and Saxton were doing that Divanni was in fact in cahoots with Morago. Plus, he somehow was connected to her family's murder as well. She didn't have concrete proof yet, but she knew they were up to something bad that would potentially harm the circle of elders.

What better way to get to know him than to chat a little while alone? But Divanni was a wolf, and wolves, as far as she was concerned, could never be trusted. Tango and Saxton could be, but no one else. The cold reminder brought on that feeling of loneliness and devastation. Then the thoughts again, that Saxton and Tango were hiding information about her identity. As she tried to figure that out, she felt some odd sensation hit her mind and then the blank thoughts. Again, she couldn't recall anything about her childhood. She swallowed hard, straightened back her shoulders and remembered why she was here.

The moment they met Donovan Kylton she recognized him as a member of the circle of elders. She would have loved to give him a piece of her mind and she thought of it as Divanni walked away from her and left her alone with Donovan.

"I don't believe we've ever met." He took her hand and kissed the top of it. She didn't miss his little sniff either. He scrunched up his nose and she had to hide the chuckle. Wearing the perfume would throw off their abilities and agitate their senses. It was just for kicks, but wouldn't disguise the fact that she was human and had were blood.

She listened in, as another two gentleman joined the conversation. She felt a thrust of awareness hit her core as the man she thought was security stood beside her. He gave her the once-over and smiled. The other one held her expression firmly with intensity. They were both very large, and well built. Her feminine instincts kicked in as thoughts of how it would feel to be held in arms so big and strong invaded her mind.

"Who's your friend, Donovan?" the big guy asked. Melena absorbed his dark crew-cut hair and gorgeous ocean-blue eyes. He was very good looking and rugged. The other man was almost identical but slightly taller. Her body immediately took notice in a totally different kind of way. Her breasts tingled, her nipples hardened, and damn it, her pussy felt so swollen. She clamped her legs together and cleared her throat. *What the hell?*

"This is Melena Zekar. Melena, meet Chordeo and Chance Dolberg."

Xavier's nephews. She'd heard about them. Xavier said they were away in Ireland helping another were pack. Why were they here? They looked like linebackers. Chordeo took her hand and brought it to his lips. As he kissed the top and held her gaze, she saw something change in his eyes. They nearly began to glow. As he pulled back, the other man, Chance, did the same thing. She started to pull her hand away, thinking that he was holding it way too long to be considered casual when the sounds of a heated argument echoed around them.

"They belong to my boss. He expects them back this evening." The one man yelled. She noticed the other man, plus two others behind him approach, looking angry.

"Tell Morago, finders keepers," the guy replied sarcastically and then chuckled. The first man didn't take the second man's comment lightly. Her ears perked up at the mention of Morago.

It was like some sort of crazy sci-fi movie. Men half shifted as they argued and began shoving one another. A thick, strong arm wrapped around her midsection, and as she grabbed the arm and tilted her head up to see who it was, there was Chordeo.

"Step back with me, Melena." His warm breath collided against her neck and the feel of his massive arms brought her instant feelings of security and lust. Her pussy seemed to swell with awareness and she damned her inexperience and virginity for having this reaction to the first sexy, muscular guy who touched her. The fact that he wasn't even human made her attempt to pry his hands from their position even more futile. But the circumstances before her took precedence of her actions. One of the men shifted and Divanni's guards began to retaliate. Chordeo released her and placed her behind him as objects flew through the room. As she attempted to escape like the other guests, someone else grabbed her.

"She was with Divanni. Bring her to the back room now," some guy ordered, and then she remembered seeing him with Filletto's man. Why would they be interested in her? Could they know who she was? She saw Divanni being pulled away and Chordeo and Chance were fighting some other guys. It was total chaos and she didn't know what was happening. As this guy pulled her along with him, she waited for the opportunity to ditch him and get the heck out of there.

"Don't put up a struggle. You're going to need your energy with the count," the man told her. She didn't know what exactly that meant, but she had a feeling it wouldn't be a good situation. She attempted to yank her arm from his grasp as he practically dragged her from the main area. There was so much other commotion going on, it appeared that the fact she was being abducted wasn't even noticed.

As they approached the hallway she twisted from his grasp then made her move. He took a few swings at her or maybe it was the goon's lame attempt at trying to nab her with his big mitts, but then she ducked and shoved him, causing him to lose his balance on the top step, fall over the railing and down the stairs to the people below.

Melena locked gazes with Chance who had seen what happened, but then she turned the other way.

Melena ran as the sounds of growls and roars filled the small venue. Where the hell was Xavier? Where could she hide or escape to until this was over? As she ran down the final hallway to another exit, she noticed the men in black. They were big and they were wolves. She abruptly turned around and smacked into a wall of steel. Big arms grabbed her shoulders and gave her a shake. She looked up into gorgeous ocean-blue eyes that glowed with specks of black.

She gasped as the surge of lust hit her gut hard.

Holy hotness. Whoever said sexy characters in books couldn't be real was fucking dead wrong.

"Get behind me and I will protect you."

The chills ran down her spine. His dark blue eyes. His deep voice, like steel hitting titanium, echoed over her flesh. He looked sort of familiar, and then it hit her. This guy looked nearly identical to Chance and Chordeo, but somehow was taller and meaner looking. He looked kind of wild with his long wavy hair hanging loose over his shoulders.

"Hand over the woman, Gideon. The count wants her with him now," one of the guys ordered.

"I don't think so, Cypress. She is with me and my brothers."

Melena felt her heart racing. *Gideon?*

What the hell was going on? How did this situation turn to such chaos? She didn't belong to any of these men. Was this what wolves did? They eyed a woman and staked a claim and that was it? No fucking way.

"I'm not anyone's possession. Let me out of here."

Before she could move away, the one called Gideon reached back and secured her body against the wall and behind his massive body with one hand. His palm was plastered across her ass and thigh, and damn did her temperature rise. She tried pushing against his huge back and felt the rumble of his growl beneath the palms of her hands.

That wild mane of hair of his smelled like soap and wilderness. She caught herself pausing and he took that as a sign of acquiescence.

"Remain where you are. These guys are bad news and you'll never make it to the count," he whispered low.

"I'm not with the fucking count, wolf," she stated back, and he growled louder, causing her to tighten up and press her shoulder against the wall.

"You're surrounded, Gideon. Just release the woman."

"Not a chance, Cypress. Why don't you come and get her."

"Are you crazy? There are five of them and one of you," she said against his back. He was so tall her face hadn't even come close to his shoulder and she was wearing six-inch heels.

She felt the rumble of his words and for some crazy reason they touched something deep within her.

"You have no fucking idea, sweetheart," Gideon whispered then turned toward her and held her gaze. She stared right back into his eyes and saw his nostrils flare and something carnal and animal-like come over him. He was breathing heavy and appeared in shock until Cypress and two others attacked.

Melena ducked and moved out of the way as Cypress literally charged Gideon and tried to tackle him to the rug. Gideon didn't even falter as he tossed Cypress off of him only to have two other wolves attack. She was completely frightened by Gideon's reaction to her. He looked like he wanted to eat her.

"Come with me." This other guy, not as big as Cypress, and his friends grabbed her arm.

"Let go of me. I'm not going anywhere with you!" she yelled as she tried to get him to release her arm.

"The count wants you to return to his estate with him. He has chosen you." The guy told her and she saw his eyes begin to glow.

"I don't think so. I'm not available." She twisted her arm from his grasp and began to run. He was on her fast as he shoved her against the wall. His face was inches from her neck.

He sniffed against her shoulder and neck as she panted for breath and the strength to fight this creep off.

"You smell so good. No wonder the count and the vamp are interested."

She was shocked. The count and the vamp? This guy licked her skin, his tongue long and wet against her flesh. Her face was turned sideways and she saw the fighting going on in the hallway. There was blood but none of the men completely shifted. She was scared and she knew she couldn't let this guy bring her to the count or to the vampire.

"I'm not going with them, but I'll go anywhere with you," she whispered as she eased her hand between them, brushing her hand across his huge cock that was pressed against his tuxedo pants. She tried not to shake. It was her first time touching a man, never mind touching his most intimate part. It seemed a lot easier to do in the books she read and while lost in a character's role. She reminded herself that she was in danger and that she was playing a role, too. If feeling this guy up was key to pulling the slip on him, then goddamn it, she was going to do it perfectly.

The man eased back and held her gaze. Oh yeah, the power of a seductive woman proved useful against a wolf. She let her thumb graze along the base and his hand came up and held her throat.

She gasped.

"The count wants to make you his latest fuck. I could get lost along the way to his estate, and we could get you ready for him."

The sick bastard. Wolves showed no loyalty to anyone but themselves. This guy was supposed to be working for the count or the vamp, whatever, and he let his own desires get in the way of his job. This was the problem with wolves and with most people. No loyalty. She moved her hand lower and her fingers brushed against the silver switchblade.

She closed her eyes and willed herself to be strong and defend herself. She needed to get the hell out of here.

"Sounds intriguing." She rolled her tongue along her lips. The growls and roars continued down the hallway. She turned and saw not only the one called Gideon, but also Chordeo and Chance.

The wolf's hand grabbed her throat tighter.

"I will kill you in one snap if you're playing games with me."

She gripped the knife as he pressed harder against her body and bared his teeth. He leaned closer, his teeth were against her neck, and she felt the pinch and feared that he was going to bite her.

"I take death very seriously, so should you."

She stuck the knife into his gut and the wolf roared as he fell backward. His wound burned and smelled horrible as a small bit of smoke rose from where she stabbed him. The stench was rancid and it caused the other wolves to remain at bay. She ran down the hallway without the knife in hand and through the exit door.

As she looked both ways, wondering which way to go, she spotted the limo with the unique license plate. As she headed that way, she felt the tug on her hand, and turning toward another mean-looking wolf, she swung her fist and hit him square in the jaw. As she tumbled into the velvet-roped fence used outside to keep the crowds in line, the other wolf attacked. She grabbed one of the brass stands. It fell apart and now was a fourteen-inch-long piece of tubular brass. She swung at him, hitting his head. He fell to the ground, and she ran toward the limo, jumped in, and released an uneasy breath as she tried to calm her breathing. She didn't know why she jumped into the limo. Just that she saw it and something told her to get in.

"Quite the party, wasn't it, Melena?"

She squealed as she opened her eyes and saw Julius.

She tried to move but the car was in motion and the doors locked.

"I don't think so. You and I have some business to discuss. Oh, and give me the makeshift weapon, before somebody gets hurt."

By no recollection of her own, Melena handed over the brass bar without further hesitation, then eased back into her seat and crossed her legs. The vampire looked over her body and licked his lips.

"It seems I have a bit of a moral dilemma on my hands. And vampires don't do moral dilemmas."

Chapter 5

"Who is she?" Gideon demanded to know.

His uncle, Xavier Dolberg, stared at him and his brothers.

"She is an associate of mine. Melena has been working for me for the last few years. I don't know why anyone would want to hurt her, unless it is to get to me. That's my only thought right now. She must be scared out of her mind."

Gideon stared at his uncle then looked at his brothers. Chordeo and Chance were just as riled up as he was. They inhaled her scent. They knew that she was their mate. By the gods, they had no idea how this could happen nor that it was even possible to have another mate after losing their first one to death.

"What does Julius want with her?" Chordeo asked as he clenched his teeth.

"I do not know. You all know him as well as I do. When he sets his sights on something, he goes after it. Melena is quite the beauty." Xavier looked at Gideon and raised his eyebrows at him. They stared at one another and Gideon spoke his mind.

"It seems that she is quite important to us as well."

"How so, Gideon?" Xavier asked, pushing for answers. "You just met her tonight."

"She is our mate," Gideon responded and Xavier uncrossed his arms and stood straighter.

"Your mate? All of you?"

"Yes," the Dolberg Pack, Gideon, Mano, Chordeo, Chance, and Edric, responded in sync.

Xavier ran his fingers through his hair then walked over toward his desk. Their uncle knew that they had lost their mate years ago. He didn't know the circumstances or who she was. They really didn't know much about her either. Just that her father was a royal in the government and often supplied information on illegal activities against the circle. It was why he had been killed.

"She is not just an associate of mine. She is my liaison. Melena is of great importance to me as well. It seems that the fates have totally shocked me with this one. You see, Melena is the mastermind behind the development of the Security Ring."

"What? I thought that was all your doing," Edric said.

"I had some good insight from Melena and she was filled with wonderful ideas. She runs the program. She runs the background checks on individuals our committee feels are suitable to become part of the Security Ring. It is only the beginning stages, but we have secured the standings of four members thus far. She has such enthusiasm and drive to protect those involved with the government and those who protect the sanctity of the circle. She wants to create a better force of communication between the Security Ring and the circle to ensure the safety of those who are innocently injured or killed during a covert operation. I swear, it amazes me that she has such drive considering that she is human, with only hints of were blood."

"What do you mean hints of were blood?" Gideon asked.

"She is not full were, nor half were. However, somewhere along her bloodline there was were blood. All I know is that I will never forget the day I met her and interviewed her for the position. She hadn't even been looking for the job, but we met by chance and we began to discuss things at the company. She fit the position perfectly and she had no family. There was no one for her to take care of or go home to, so she submerged herself in the job and in the position as my liaison."

"That's why we've never seen her before?" Mano asked.

"Yes. She works in a private location and office. She prefers that."

"And who are these members of this Security Ring, uncle?" Chordeo asked.

"How can a human woman be allowed to be in such a position? She isn't even of the wolf. There must be more to Julius's interest in her," Mano stated.

"I do not know why Julius has taken her. I do know that both Divanni and Filletto's men showed interest, too. They could have been challenging one another. I'll get to the bottom of it. If you'll excuse me." Xavier exited the room.

"We need to do something about this," Chance stated.

"We will. Let's go pay the vamp a visit and secure our mate," Gideon said and they nodded their heads then headed out of the office. He was trying to sift through the information they had about her thus far. They wouldn't let their mate get away or get injured before they could protect her. Losing one mate was enough pain to last their lifetime.

* * * *

Melena kept her legs crossed and her hands clasped on her lap as the limo driver continued to drive south. She stared at the vamp, wondering what he wanted with her as his eyes held hers. When the darkness overtook the cabin of the vehicle, his eyes shone red and she swallowed hard. She wasn't as prepared as she thought she would be, meeting a vampire like Julius. She was trying to remember what she was taught about vampires without projecting her thoughts toward the vampire. He squinted his eyes and she wondered if she was successful or not. It seemed to her that it was easier to talk and ask the questions than think about them first. She wanted to know where they were going and what exactly he wanted with her. Like it wasn't enough that some serious criminal wolves wanted her in their bed tonight?

"So, what exactly is the moral dilemma you were speaking of?" she asked him as the driver headed onto the highway illuminated by numerous streetlights. In a flash he was sitting beside her. She gasped, taken aback by his quick move.

His hand covered her hand.

"Sweet, sweet Melena. You do not know who you really are, but I do. I sensed it almost immediately. I'm rather surprised that Xavier allowed you to even attend such an event with so many enemies around. Unless, he has no idea. Interesting."

Fear hit her gut immediately. Could this vampire know more about her than she knew herself?

"What are you talking about?"

"Ah, I must say that your trainers have done well. Your ability to stab a dangerous wolf with a silver blade shows gall and strength. I like that in my women." He reached up to caress her cheek and his fingers trailed along her jaw. She felt that odd sensation of warmth and calmness begin to relax her body. Unknowingly, she eased against him, until her mind cleared.

Pulling back and scooting away from him, she glared.

"I don't think so, vamp. I'm not some easy prey and I do not like having my mind and emotions tampered with. Tell me what you want."

He took a deep breath and released it softly.

He stared down into her eyes as he caressed her jaw with his fingers. It was as if he were memorizing her features.

"I think, I would like to keep you. I mean, not as a prisoner, but more."

"Not happening," she retorted just as the sound of a cell phone rang. Julius answered the call.

"Hello, Xavier. I was expecting your call. Seems I have someone of interest to you and your pack. She was in great danger of being taken by the enemy."

Melena listened in and hoped that Xavier could get this vampire to release her. She wasn't sure if he would do her harm, yet there was this sensation of a connection to him. He was very attractive, despite his pasty coloring.

He looked at her and winked. *Could he read my mind?*

She had never met Julius Kordosky, but had lots of information on him. This had to be him. Xavier never mentioned any other vampires of interest except for one mated to Dani and Fagan Pack. That must be something wild. All those big, feisty men and a vampire. She shook her head. This wasn't happening. She didn't belong here right now. None of their rituals or rules applied to her.

"I'm not sure that is a good idea. Wolves can be so savage like. She is precious and sophisticated. I think I'll keep her in safekeeping until you can meet me."

He closed up the phone and leaned back into the seat.

"There is much for us to discuss. You should be relieved that I saved you from those wolves."

"I saved myself," she stated with attitude.

He smiled.

"I wasn't talking about the wolf you killed. I was talking about the wolves who claim you to be their mate."

She was shocked as she felt her jaw drop.

"I am not the mate to anyone."

He raised his eyebrows at her. She couldn't help but think there was more to his statement and he was hesitating.

"Seems Xavier's nephews think otherwise. I for one do not like to share. You would be much better off with me and well taken care of, my goddess."

He leaned in and moved his mouth gently across her neck. She felt her head lean back as she tilted her neck and gave him better access to her throat. His lips were surprisingly warm for a vampire. His kisses were soft, appealing, and she felt something deep within her react to him. But then came the images of the wolves and the information Julius gave her.

Julius nipped her skin then licked across the flesh.

She gasped as she thought about Chordeo, Chance, and the one called Gideon.

Her belly tightened and she felt the attraction to them even in her mind. It couldn't be true. She pulled away from his hold, and his eyes looked so intense she knew she could never physically fight a vampire like Julius. She also realized that she didn't want to. He smirked and she felt embarrassed. She changed the subject as his hand glided up her calf to her thigh and the slit of the dress that showed off her tan legs.

"Three wolves as my mates? You are insane. I am human and I don't follow the same ideas and rules as wolves or vampires. You should just let me off at the next exit."

She turned to look out the window and to figure out where they could possibly be and how she could escape.

"Five. Alpha wolves, sweetheart."

She widened her eyes. There were five of those big guys? Five men who decided that they wanted her as their mate or whatever.

"Not happening." She crossed her arms and leaned back in the seat.

He chuckled.

"I think this is going to be fun to watch. But know this, I won't give you up so easily. You'll need me, eventually."

She wasn't sure what Julius meant by that comment but as the limo eased off the highway and toward an upscale development, she saw the black SUV and five huge men standing there in tuxedos.

The limo stopped and Julius waited for the driver to open his door. She could see the intense expressions of the five monstrosities. She knew what they were capable of. One on one, perhaps she would have a fighting chance to escape, but five on one and the help of some crazy vampire and she was doomed. She hadn't worked this hard and sacrificed so much to be taken down by these six men.

Her heart pounded inside her chest and Julius turned to her. He winked as the driver opened his door and Julius stepped out first. The vampire was being smug and in his act of pissing off the wolves, Melena made her move.

She closed the door, climbed over the driver's seat, and was behind the wheel.

She placed the running vehicle in drive and sped off down the driveway. As the front gates began to close, she floored the gas pedal and took out the gates as she skidded sideways onto the main street. In the rearview mirror she saw the vampire chuckling and the wolves scattering toward the vehicle as they growled at the vamp.

Melena never eased off the gas pedal. When she saw what looked like the perfect spot to ditch the vehicle she did. She glanced around the darkness and the streets in front of her. As the long gray bus appeared from the distance, she saw the one woman standing near a bench with a bus stop sign beside it. Quickly she crossed the street and nibbled her bottom lip as she awaited the bus. In the distance coming from the direction of the vampire's house she saw nothing but darkness. Finally, the bus approached and stopped. She hopped onto the commuter bus and eased down into a seat way in the back.

As the bus slowed near a red light, she saw the black SUV heading into the direction she just came from. She made it out of there by the skin of her teeth. Her next move was to get back home and interrogate the shit out of Saxton and Tango.

Chapter 6

"What do you mean she got away and she killed Phillip with a silver knife?" Count Divanni asked as he stood in his study, wearing his silk robe as he waited for the beautiful blonde to be delivered to him.

"She was tougher than expected. She fought Phillip off and it seems that the Dolberg Pack is showing interest in her as well," Colin explained.

"Dolberg Pack? What the fuck? She's human with a hint of were blood, a nothing, a nobody aside from her hot body and charming appeal. She will look amazing on my arm wherever we go. Find her. Find out everything you can about her and get her to me. I'll take care of that asshole wolf of Filletto's. Oh, better yet, send Bartholomy, to have a little chat with Lance. Let him know that as count, I am not bowing down to his Alpha, Filletto. The man should know that. After all, I do hold the power to get their operation in motion to destroy the circle. There are plans to complete, starting with the destruction of the Collette family. Mercer Collette must be stopped before he figures out about the United Shield and our plans."

"I'm on it, Count," Colin stated, bowed, then left the room.

Count Divanni eased back against the desk.

By sending his enforcer, Bartholomy, to speak firmly with Lance, Filletto's main Alpha wolf, Divanni could focus on finding out more about Melena. Mercer Collette had a lot of pull in the circle of elders. He could influence many members and had shown such capability in the past. Mercer needed a little pressure, too, now.

"I was hoping to share my bed with you tonight, Melena, but I guess you will be more of a challenge than I thought. Very interesting indeed." The count walked around to his desk and picked up the phone.

"Get me everything you can on Melena Zekar and her job at the city council. Place some men on Xavier Dolberg and his nephews. I want to know their every move and the moment that Melena is found."

* * * *

As Melena entered the security door Saxton and Tango were standing there. "So, how did it go?"

"You want to know how it went? It was a nightmare!" she exclaimed as she approached, but before she could go off and explain what happened, both men grabbed her and sniffed her. Saxton looked at Tango.

"Julius Kordosky?"

"Dolberg wolves," Tango added.

She pulled her arm fee.

"Some serious shit went down and how the hell can you tell whom I was with by smelling me?"

"He touched you?" Tango asked with teeth clenched.

She swallowed hard.

Saxton grabbed her hand and pulled her into a hug. He growled low then brought her into the living room.

"Tell us what happened," Tango said.

"It was a mess." As she came to the part about the fight breaking out, they immediately became concerned.

"We should have never allowed this. They know who you are. Somehow they sniffed it out." Saxton raised his voice as she stood up and began pacing the room.

"Sniffed what out? That I'm mostly human with possibly a bit of were blood in me? Is that some kind of commodity or delicacy or something? Because Julius was all over me, and when he licked my neck, I felt something and then there were the wolves. Dolberg Pack. Holy shit, are they huge men and good looking, in a very rugged, rip your fucking body apart with my bare hands or claws or whatever."

"What did you say? Julius licked your neck?" Saxton asked.

She lowered her eyes and felt her cheeks warm.

"Melena!"

"Oh God, he sort of rescued me I think. I mean I was running after I stabbed the jackass wolf with the silver switchblade. Which, I left there by accident. I hope they don't find my fingerprints on it. That was crazy, his skin practically exploded and the smell, the smell was disgusting."

"You killed a wolf?" Tango raised his voice.

"I had no choice. He was about to bite me then bring me to the count, who supposedly had chosen me to be, as the wolf stated, the count's fuck for the night. I was just defending myself."

"Fuck!" Saxton yelled.

"That's what the guy said, not me," she retorted with attitude.

Both men looked so enraged.

"Hey, I'm the one who is totally freaked out here. I mean, there were all these wolves, half shifting and roaring at one another. The next thing I know I'm meeting three men from Dolberg Pack and they're sniffing my hand and staring at me with hunger in their eyes. I fear they want to eat me, so I start to think it's time to go when this fight breaks out. Some guy connected to Filletto or the count grabs me. Then another guy does, as all this chaos is happening and so I stabbed the bad wolf in order to get away before he bit me or could abduct me for the count. As I'm running out of there, Dolberg Pack is growling but can't seem to pass the wolf with the silver wound. I hurry out, get this urge to go to the limo parked there and get in, but it must have been the vampire powers, because when I get inside, Julius is there. He's speaking all cryptic and he's whispering in my ear and then tells me that the Dolberg Pack believe me to be their mate. Can you believe that shit?" She stood up and began to pace as both Tango and Saxton looked ready to explode in anger.

"Dolberg Pack? There are fucking five of those Alpha males. They're animals," Tango exclaimed.

"Tell me about it. Then Julius says he's interested in me and not about to let me go so easily. He was trying to mind control me, too. And he nearly was successful as he licked my neck and well, just, he was close to manipulating my mind but I stopped him somehow. The moment we arrived at his estate or whatever, the Dolberg Pack were there and they looked pissed off."

"Oh shit. What did you do? How the hell did you escape?" Tango asked.

"As soon as the vamp got out of the car, I jumped over the divider, got into the driver's seat because the car was running, and I took off. I ditched the car and hopped on the bus and here I am. What an outrageous night."

Melena stared at both men who appeared to be in shock until Saxton pulled her into his arms and hugged her.

"We have a lot to do. Tango and I have some decisions to make."

"Decisions about what?"

"Your future. We need to get that knife back and secure your identity."

"Good luck with that, Saxton. The place was swarming with big shots."

"I'll take care of it. You better shower and get rid of that stench on you."

* * * *

"She stabbed a wolf with a silver blade, she escaped from a vampire, and she stole a limo, ditched it and somehow got away from us, where we can't track her. I'm in love already," Edric stated toward his brothers who sat around their living room feeling frustrated and annoyed. Gideon was on the phone trying to get Xavier to give up more info on their mate.

"It is impressive. Considering that hot, sexy body and that tight dress she was wearing, she appeared well trained. Where could she be hiding?" Chance asked.

"I've got this feeling that just like our entire lives have been complicated and crazy, so will be capturing our mate and getting her to trust us. She's running for a reason," Mano said.

"She is human. Our first mate was of the wolf," Chordeo added.

"She is more than that. We sensed were blood, though faint, and this time, we will secure our mate," Chance added.

Gideon entered the room.

"We have to find her. Xavier is very concerned. Members of both Divanni's pack and Filletto's pack are searching for her and trying to get information from our uncle. I'm glad we secured the knife before Filletto or the count's men could. That wolf she stabbed was a wanted man anyway," Gideon said.

"She came prepared for the unexpected. Why else would she be carrying a silver knife like that?" Mano asked.

"There has to be good reason. Xavier hasn't given me much, but I suspect this woman Melena is hiding her identity for a reason," Gideon added.

"Well, that isn't going to be for long Gideon. The count and Filletto are resourceful. They'll figure out who she is, just as quickly as we will. We need to find her first," Edric stated.

"The count and Filletto are being cordial now, but we know how those assholes operate. I will not stand by and allow another mate to be killed. We must protect her," Gideon said.

"Yeah, and because of some other secret reasons, we're not allowed to take those assholes out. How many fucking innocent people need to be hurt and killed before the circle gives the order to eliminate them?" Chordeo asked and everyone was quiet and in agreement.

"We have to find her. There's more, too," Gideon said.

"What more?" Edric asked.

"Julius has an interest in her."

"Fuck! Is this going to be like Dani and our cousins in Fagan Pack, where we must share a mate with a vamp? Because that is not fucking happening," Chance said loudly.

They all growled low.

"Let's not jump to conclusions. We'll speak with Julius. He more than likely will find Melena before any of us anyway. Plus we have business to discuss with him. Mano is going to work on finding out about a possible secret society trying to plan an attack on the elders," Gideon said.

"What? When did you get this information?" Chordeo asked.

"He got it before leaving for the gala. I don't have anything yet. My mind can't seem to focus on anything but finding our mate," Mano stated.

"Doesn't Xavier have a home address on her?" Edric asked. "She is an employee and she's working on something pretty damn important."

"She's been secretive from the start. Our uncle believes this is because of her lack of family. She's obsessed with work and developing the Security Ring. He did confirm that she has were blood and that she was highly recommended by two higher-ups in the government," Gideon said.

"Two higher-ups? I bet if we can find out who they are, then we can find out where to find our mate," Edric stated and they all mumbled in agreement.

"Hopefully the two higher-ups are not on the list of potential threats we were given by Dani and Van. This has the components to become volatile very quickly," Gideon said and they all agreed.

* * * *

It didn't take long for him to find her. Julius was determined to learn more about Melena and her life. When he had first seen her face, he had done a double take. She was the spitting image of Llana Mahalan. A beautiful Polynesian woman who had been married to Zeikele Mahalan, a leader of the protectors of the circle. He and his family had been brutally murdered to the point that their bodies, except for Zeikele, had been ripped to shreds. He thought his mind had been playing tricks on him, but then he saw Kamea across the room at the party and was shocked. As he moved closer, gained her scent, the suspicion that the Mahalan child had survived became believable. He still hadn't been certain until he licked across her skin and felt the intense attraction.

When she was a child, he had been instantly aware of her and protective. Julius sighed in recognition as he waited on the top of the building. She was only twelve at the time but as he saw her only months before the attack, he felt the connection and he knew that she was of importance to him. He didn't dare speak his thoughts to her parents. Zeikele was a very calm and smart wolf, but he would not want his only daughter to end up mated to a vampire and living forever. Zeikele found out about Julius's protectiveness over Kamea and forbid him to come near her ever again. Now, it seemed that the gods had played another one of their wild and crazy tricks. Melena, who was really Kamea, was not only destined to be mated to a vampire, but also five very crazy, robust Alpha wolves, destined for greatness.

Julius needed to tread carefully. He had made a promise to Zeikele that he couldn't break, despite his connection to her. Even now, as she slept, he felt her presence from afar. She was indeed of great importance to him but she was also in a heap of trouble. He wondered who had helped the child escape and how the heck had she survived anyway? As he made himself invisible he got his answer to at least one of his questions. He sniffed the air and recognized the scent of wolves. Two in particular he knew rather well from many years ago. Now he knew why Tango and Saxton disappeared. They were caring for Kamea.

Julius made his way into her bedroom. His sleeping beauty lay in hardly any clothes at all. A flimsy white tank top that barely covered large, luscious breasts and loose boxers in hot pink that made her tan complexion stand out. He eased his way over discovering that she in fact was not a blonde but a brunette, with long, flowing chocolate locks that currently cascaded along the pillows.

Her lips were full and pink, her cheekbones high and the definition in her arms and legs was that of a woman who took working out and training very seriously. He could crack eggs on her abs.

He had the urge to touch her, to arouse her body and make her acknowledge their connection. He felt the need to possess her first, because he knew that five other men were destined to have her. A promise was a promise, but like this, in this invisible form, he could touch her, feel her, without anyone knowing.

He used his mind to deliver his desire. What started out as gentle caresses across her soft, supple skin, turned into fire.

It had shocked him when her eyes popped open.

"Julius?" she asked then tried to sit up.

"How?" He appeared before her, no longer invisible. He sat down beside her on the bed. She looked so innocent and lovely.

"You felt me? You knew it was me?" he asked as she sat up on the bed. She stared at him with beautiful green eyes. She was fully in awe and aware of his presence. He was in awe of her power and strength.

She shook her head then slowly licked her lower lip. As the tip of her tongue collided with her lip, he felt his cock harden and he moaned softly. Melena widened her eyes.

"Why are you here? What do you want?"

He tried to calm his breathing as he used his mind control to ease her fear.

"You, Melena. I want you. I needed to find you, to talk with you and to touch you."

She closed her eyes as he used his mind to softly caress her skin. Lowering back down to the bed she opened her eyes and held his gaze.

"This is insane. I don't know you. I don't believe in vampires."

He chuckled low and she gasped as if the sound did something to her. It must have, because suddenly she opened her thighs wider and ran the palms of her hands from her throat, down over her breasts, to her pussy.

"Oh God, I feel like this is right. I want to feel you touch me. I don't know you though. Are you doing this to me? Are you making me act this way?"

He shook his head in denial.

"My beautiful creature. I could take advantage of you without you knowing if I wanted to. But it seems, like no other, you have the ability to stop me from doing anything against your will. It is like we are connected beyond anything I have ever felt dear to. My blood is pumping through my veins, almost calling out to your blood, your scent, and your body."

She began to breathe more rapidly as she tilted her head back, parted her lips, and sighed in recognition.

"I feel it, Julius. Holy shit, I can feel it. I want to scream with need. This is not right. How can you do this to me?"

"Don't scream. Don't be fearful. I would never cause you harm." He ran a finger across her breasts and she gasped.

"Julius, I don't even know you and you're a vampire." She chuckled slightly as if in disbelief of not only the words leaving her lips but the emotion she was feeling.

"But that's not how I operate. I want you to feel my touch, to want more of me. It's how I feel about you."

He made soft circles over her nipple and areola, and the fabric pushed out as her nipple hardened.

"Yes. Touch me. Do something to ease this ache," she whispered then closed her eyes.

Her legs parted, she rolled to her back, and tilted her chin upward. In her current state, she moaned softly as he played gently with her breasts. Her lips parted.

Oh what I would do for a kiss from your lips, a taste of your cream, a chant of desire from your heart.

He felt the urge to resist. Just one more peek at his gorgeous Polynesian goddess. Just one more touch. It wasn't right to do this. Not now, not when he promised to restrain his need.

"Please, Julius. You know what to do. You have to. You're a vampire, an experienced man. Why does everything ache? Why am I not frightened of you?"

The poor woman doesn't even know how it works. She is destined as my mate, yet I cannot consummate the joining. Not when I made such a promise so many years ago. But I can bring her pleasure. Even if only from my touch and not by joining our bodies as one.

"Are you sure, Melena?"

She nodded her head.

"Help me, Julius. I want to feel your hands on me."

"Close your eyes."

She did as he told her, like a good mate should. His heart ached for that bond with her, but knowing that the five wolves shared the same fate with her brought him a mix of emotions. He was angry, jealous but also relieved that she would be well taken care of. The Dolberg wolves were resourceful men. Their hardened hearts would not remain so cold and hard for long.

He, too, closed his eyes and allowed his body to take whatever form it needed to. It felt as if he were justifying the need to have her, and being invisible would seem like the best alternative. Technically, it wouldn't count as breaking his promise. *Technically.*

Her shorts moved down her hips, revealing her perfectly shaved and pink pussy to his eyes. He inhaled her scent as she thrust her hips upward.

Invisible, he lay by her side, trailing a finger along her curves, imagining being inside of her, making love to her and binding them for life.

"Julius, where are you?" she asked in a voice that quivered, making his cock harden and his need to fuck her become almost impossible to resist. But he couldn't. He couldn't let this go so far. He shouldn't even be here now, but she was his mate. The man, the vampire needed this connection, like he needed breath and blood.

Her legs parted wider, his thoughts, his desires leading him to take more. His blood pushed toward the surface and reacted in finding its mate but the promise to her father held the reins tight. He inhaled more of Kamea's scent. Her glistening cunt teased his hunger similarly to the need and thirst for blood and he could not control the desire to take a taste.

Just one lick of her pussy, her cream and he would leave her alone. He delved his tongue between the wet folds as she panted and gasped. Her hands reached down to cover her pussy but he controlled her mind, her movements as her arms shot upward and against the pillow. The move caused her breasts to push forward and he caressed them with nimble fingers as he ate at her cream. She was so delicious. Such a tasty treat that he couldn't stop. The fact that he knew she had the power to stop him but chose to be submissive and allow him these ministrations immersed pride through his entire being.

"Julius! Oh my goodness, that feels so good."

He smiled.

"More?" he asked between licks.

"Yes. Yes, more." She thrust her hips upward.

He needed more, too. His fangs nipped along her clitoris and she moaned louder. Her body tightened and he calmed her mind, her voice so she wouldn't cry out when she came. Her entire body sprung tight as he licked and sucked then took a little bite against the vein by her groin. She exploded, her body convulsed as she sat up gasping for air.

* * * *

Melena was breathing heavy, panting like some wild woman. She was dreaming of a man's touch, a vampire's touch, when she suddenly awoke and saw Julius. She thought he was in her dreams, but then he spoke to her, told her that he wanted to touch her. She didn't need to think twice. She wanted it, too. For some god forsakenly strange reason, it was like she knew it was right. She knew that letting Julius touch her, taste her, fuck her would be right and oh so good. But she had the feeling that he wouldn't go so far. Once she gave him permission, he used his mind to ease her concern and to also lower her voice. God, she wanted to scream out in ecstasy but couldn't. It was such an amazing feeling. It was so sexual, so bold and strong the way he restrained her body and mind while bringing her pleasure but also giving her part of him.

She felt lost in his strokes. The way his long tongue devoured her cream and made her pussy swollen for more of the sensations. At that moment she would give him whatever he wanted. As her breathing grew rapid and her hips thrust up toward his tongue and mouth, she felt some kind of magnetic force. It shocked her and made her become completely still but then, he bit her. She began to awaken fully as she looked around the dark room, wondering what the hell just happened. As she looked down she saw that she no longer wore her boxers and her pussy felt swollen and needy. She felt the cream dripping from her as she reached down and touched her pussy lips. The fear and excitement rushed through her system.

"Julius? Show yourself again. I wanted this. I asked for you to touch me like this. Please, let me see you again?" As the words passed her lips, fear gripped her insides and sadness that he was afraid to stay. He didn't do anything wrong. It felt so right.

He was here with her. First right beside her on the bed and then invisible as he touched her intimately. She gave him permission. She allowed it, relished in it and wanted more.

So much fucking more. But he left me. Why would he leave me? Was it nothing to him?

She pulled on her boxers as she stared around the room wondering if the vampire was there. Could he really remain invisible and not talk to her about what just happened? Why was she feeling insulted? She wanted to hit something. She wanted more of Julius. *Damn it!*

"Julius? Why?" she whispered.

She jumped as she felt his hand gently glide up and down her left arm. He heart raced.

"Julius?" she whispered.

"Shh, please, Kamea. I can't. I want too much," he whispered.

"Show yourself, Julius. Let me see you."

"I should go." She gasped and shook her head as she knelt on the bed.

"Please, Julius."

It was the most amazing thing she had ever seen. First there was nothing but thin air, yet his soft, gentle touch. Then suddenly, he was there, sitting beside her on the bed, holding her arms as he stared down into her eyes.

"Sweet, precious woman. I don't know why I allowed myself to taste you, to touch you. I need to go." He released her arms. She grabbed at him and pulled him back. She didn't know why, but Melena hugged him tight, inhaled his scent and the feelings of masculinity, protectiveness of his strong, magical embrace.

"I know this is crazy. God, I feel like I've lost my mind, but I want you to come back to me, Julius. I want to see you again. Will I? Will you remain a stranger in the night?"

He stared down into her eyes and his red eyes glowed gently. They were mesmerizing. She lay back down and he scooted closer, almost over her. She swallowed hard. She felt the intense panic that he would leave and never return. Desperation filled her up.

He leaned down and kissed her forehead.

"The night, the darkness is my eternal tomb, Kamea. I dare not ruin your life with my burden." Before she could argue against his statement, she felt him ease her mind as he kissed along her throat embellishing her skin with magical, tiny kisses. When their lips touched, that fire began to burn again in her belly and straight to her pussy.

He released her lips.

"Sleep now, Kamea. Rest."

"Will you come back?" she asked, feeling groggy and exhausted, yet that ache in her pussy was still present.

"We will see," he whispered.

She closed her eyes and fell back to sleep.

Chapter 7

Julius Kordosky wasn't the least surprised to find Gideon Dolberg waiting for him at his estate.

"I was wondering if you were actually home and not answering your door on purpose or if you were out trying to locate my mate?" Gideon stated with arms crossed in front of his massive chest. Julius had a lot of respect for Gideon Dolberg and his brothers. They were quite impressive in appearance as both men and in were form.

Julius chuckled.

"Now, why, my good friend Gideon, would I ignore your calling? I was simply out enjoying the evening."

He gave a small wave and the front door unlocked. Thoughts of Kamea filled Julius's mind. The scent of her arousal, her acceptance of his touch, then how she wanted him to stay, made his mind soar with pride, but his heart ache with pain. He could not pursue her. It seemed her fate lay elsewhere with the wolves.

"Please come in." Julius motioned for Gideon to follow. The wolf sniffed the air then made a small growl.

"You saw her. You were with her again?" Gideon stepped toward Julius when Cullen, Julius's friend and caretaker, a wolf, emerged. He carried a tray holding two snifters of brandy.

"Good evening, Cullen. You remember Gideon Dolberg, don't you?" Julius headed toward the sitting room off of the main entryway and both men followed.

Cullen brought the tray over toward Gideon first.

"Brandy, sir?"

Gideon gave Julius an annoyed expression but thanked Cullen before taking the snifter. Cullen approached Julius and Julius took the other snifter as he held Cullen's gaze.

"Eventful evening, sir?"

"Very, Cullen. Perhaps you would like to join us? Grab a cognac for yourself."

"I'm good, sir, and you have only but about thirty minutes until sunrise."

"Ah, yes, my impeding bedtime despite my three hundred years of age."

"You saw her tonight again and I want to know why and where she is. She is our mate, Julius. What the hell is going on?" Gideon asked.

Julius took a sip from his drink as Cullen placed the tray down then stood by the door.

"She is in good hands, wolf."

"If she is not in my hands or my brothers', then she is not."

"It seems that the fates have given us quite the interesting adventure. You see, your mate cannot be exposed to the public eye so soon. She is of great value to the circle of elders."

"You mean because of her insight and development of the project she is engaged in with the city council?"

Julius smiled.

"I know of Xavier's development of his new security program. I am meeting him tomorrow night, to discuss my role."

"Your role? Are you out of your mind, Julius? It is a were organization completely run by loyal weres."

Julius raised his eyebrow at Gideon's insult. As if weres were more powerful or respected than vampires. Weres feared vampires because like Alpha weres, vampires were not easily controlled and many were only loyal to themselves.

"I do not mean to insult you. We have not had any problems in the past, and you do not need me to tell you about the protocol of this realm or others. On earth, the weres rule. Yes, we do branch out to other resources from time to time to ensure that the sanctity of the circle remains intact."

"Yes, your cousins in Fagan Pack are the perfect example."

Gideon ground his teeth and stared at Julius.

"That was a different situation. Vanderlan and my cousins share their mate and it ensures her healing powers and protection of the circle."

"Exactly. I am certain that Melena will present herself to you when the time is right."

Gideon placed the drink down onto the side table.

"Julius, she is our mate. You know where she is hiding and I must insist that you share this information with me and my brothers immediately. She does not belong to you. You cannot withhold information about our mate from us."

Julius rose from his seat as Cullen took the empty glasses and placed them onto the tray.

"Wait until noontime. You will find her by contacting your uncle. Melena will be communicating with him then."

"I know that something more is going on here. Is there another reason why you are not sharing her location with me now and why I can smell her scent on you?" Gideon asked.

Julius could see his friend's eyes beginning to glow. Gideon was obviously trying not to change forms. Julius wouldn't be able to lie for much longer about their fate and the fact that Melena was his mate as well.

Julius thought about it a moment. He had the opportunity to taste her, to absorb her cream, her blood, her sexuality and he wanted more. He knew that he would seek her out again and the thought of these other men doing the same while he slept angered him.

"There is no other reason, except to protect her from unidentifiable enemies."

"If you were any other vampire, I would not be accepting this so easily. However, if what you say is not true and I do not have her in my possession by tomorrow, noontime, then you and I are going to have ourselves an unfortunate situation. Enjoy your sleep." Gideon walked out of the room and Cullen escorted him to the door.

Julius sighed in annoyance. He knew it wasn't right of him to deny the Alpha and his brothers access to their mate, but he was jealous, envious, and needy for more of Kamea. He hated the fact that he had promised her father that he would remain away from her. Zeikele was too good of a friend to betray. Julius's eternal life as a vampire could not be pushed onto a woman as lovely and special as Kamea. It seemed he had some arrangements to make and protection to provide for his intended mate. Gideon and his brothers had become quite wild and powerful over the year. Getting Kamea to commit could prove to be quite the fight. Julius shook his head. The gods had the ultimate power. But he did sense some sort of magic around Kamea. Was that how she was protected from detection? he wondered then knew he needed to head to the vault. The sun would rise soon and he would have to wait until the evening to get his answers.

* * * *

Melena walked into the kitchen to find Saxton and Tango waiting for her. She sat down, placing her legs underneath her butt then pushed her long brown hair over her shoulder.

"You look exhausted," Saxton pointed out.

"I didn't sleep very well."

"No wonder, after all the excitement last night. We have some things to go over," Tango said then walked over to the coffeepot and poured her a cup.

He brought over the mug and Saxton pushed the sugar bowl then milk toward her.

She sat back, allowing the aroma of the coffee to fill her nostrils. Her belly tightened and then thoughts of her sleepless night filled her mind. The way she felt, the way her body was strung so tight, she knew she needed answers, but would she be opening up a can of worms if she spoke freely to Saxton and Tango? What choice did she have?

"Xavier called. Three times." Saxton spoke and she could hear the frustration and concern in his tone.

"Do I still have a job?"

Saxton and Tango stared at her. Saxton seemed surprised.

"Why would you go back there? You're safest here with us until we can figure out what the hell the count and Filletto wanted with you," Tango stated.

"They wanted sex. Filletto's guy told me straight out." She replied so matter-of-factly it seemed to upset Saxton. He stood up, paced the small area between the table and counter then stared at her.

"Damn it, Melena, you just don't get it. It's not like in your storybook romances. It's not pleasurable or meaningful unless it's with someone you care about and love," he told her.

She immediately thought about Julius and the way he made her feel last night. She shook her head in denial. *A vampire? Like my life is not fucked up enough?*

"When you make love to someone, it leaves an imprint on your soul. You don't need to use your body to get the answers and revenge you seek. You need to be smart and use your mind," Tango said.

"The only problem with your statement is that I will not be able to choose my lover. Your sick, fucked-up were rules have reared their ugly head and now five overlarge Alpha wolves believe me to be their mate, their personal fuck toy. Well, that is not going to happen."

"You have no control over your destiny," Saxton said.

"Bullshit I don't. I'm not allowing a group of individuals, who did nothing to protect my family or myself, to dictate my future. Screw that shit." She raised her voice and banged her hand onto the table.

"The fates have chosen for you. It is part of the reasoning behind you surviving that day and Saxton and I protecting you and training you."

"Is it also the same reason why you keep my true identity even from me?"

She felt so annoyed. It was like there were these imaginary binds holding her back, restraining her from making her own choices.

Saxton looked at Tango then to Melena.

"You know we have always done what we felt was best for you. We must stick to the plan. This could be some smoke screen and revealing your identity too soon could make matters worse," Saxton said.

She rolled her eyes in annoyance. It wasn't like she was important to the survival of the circle. She was a minor piece in an extremely large and complicated puzzle.

Julius, the vampire, popped into her head. She eased herself back down into the chair then took a sip from her coffee.

"Tell me about Julius."

It was quite clear they appeared taken aback at her statement Saxton crunched his eyebrows at her.

"He is not in your destiny," Saxton said.

"He is dangerous, Melena. He has no allegiance to anyone but himself," Tango added.

She held Saxton's gaze then lowered her eyes as she ran the tip of her finger along the ceramic rim of the mug.

"It seems that I can't get him out of my mind."

"Well get him out of your mind. He has the power to destroy you," Saxton said.

"I felt him last night, while I was sleeping."

"Was he there? In your room?" Tango asked with teeth clenched as his face began to redden.

"I'm not certain, but I felt him," she lied. Boy was he there. She could still feel him somehow.

"Bastard!" Saxton stated.

"He probably snuck into her room in one of his many forms," Tango said toward Saxton.

"What do you mean?" she asked.

"Vampires are very powerful and resourceful beings. Julius is old, experienced, and accustomed to taking whatever he wants no matter what the consequence."

"He didn't look old, Saxton." She remembered his dark hair and strikingly handsome features and of course, his long, thick fingers as they stroked her breasts and her cunt. He had large wide shoulders and a slim waist. Even though he was sort of pale looking, he was appealing and she had felt the attraction to him immediately. As she thought of him now, she felt the tiny goose bumps travel along her skin. She couldn't help but wonder if he were here, in the room right now.

She looked around the room, and Saxton and Tango seemed to follow her line of thinking.

"He is not here now," Saxton stated.

"How do you know?"

"We would smell his stench from a mile away," Tango added with attitude.

Well you didn't smell it last night and both of you were right next door.

She didn't dare egg them on. It seemed that Saxton and Tango were quite angry right now. But she did have more questions.

"I want to know more about him. I feel he is of importance to this operation. Last night he appeared in the crowd and he and the others spoke of an exchange. He may somehow be connected to those missing jewels. Julius was sporting a mighty fine pendant below his black jacket."

"You see what we mean about him being dangerous? For all we know he could be assisting Morago right now," Tango said.

"I don't think so. He was annoyed but not overly angry. More like inconvenienced. When I was alone with him, in his limo, he mentioned a moral dilemma."

Saxton and Tango exchanged glances.

"I wouldn't worry about Julius. Once your mates get a hold of you, no other men will be allowed near you." Saxton poured his cup of coffee down the drain.

That statement really angered her. Especially after allowing Julius to touch her so intimately last night. She wanted to see him again. She didn't want anything to do with Dolberg Pack or their animalistic desires.

"As I mentioned earlier, that is not going to happen. Now, I would like more information on the vamp and the Dolberg Pack. If I am going to evade them, then I need to know everything I can about them. First, I will call Xavier." She stood up and walked toward the sink.

Tango took her hand and the minute he was shoulder to shoulder with her he inhaled. His eyes scrunched up and he stared at her in an odd way. She felt immediately guilty and on the defensive.

"What?"

"Nothing. Go get ready, make the call and then we'll discuss the plan."

She walked away feeling like Saxton looked at her differently than ever before.

* * * *

"What was wrong?" Tango asked Saxton after Melena left the room.

"I fucking smelled the vamp on her. I smelled Julius and I don't like where the scent became stronger."

Tango widened his eyes.

"Do you think he took advantage of her while she slept?"

"He did something and she felt it. Why do you think she had all those questions about Julius and not her mates?"

"Fuck, Saxton. Like it's not bad enough that Melena is mate to those ginormous men, but now a vampire, Julius, no less, is interested in her. Her father was concerned about this years ago. I thought he had threatened Julius? What are we going to do?"

"Zeikele warned Julius away from his daughter because he thought Julius was only interested in staking a claim to the circle by joining the family bloodline. Julius has proven himself of good nature for decades. That was Zeikele being overprotective and suspicious of everyone. We may just need to allow her mates to handle this. It will be their job anyway, once she seals the mating bond with them. Let's do what we can to protect her while she is still under our protection. You know Melena as well as I do. This is not going to go smoothly at all."

"How can you give her up so easily, Saxton? When I think about Dolberg Pack and how crazy those wolves are, it concerns me. Melena is tough, but she is not an Alpha wolf. Gideon and Edric are huge and their tempers and attitudes are—"

"All Alpha, the way they should be. Mano, Chordeo, and Chance are no different. If that's who the gods have chosen for her, then there isn't anything we can do about it."

"You think Melena is going to accept this just because these wolves tell her it is so?"

Saxton shook his head then snorted.

"Those wolves are in for hell. Melena doesn't abide by her ancestors' rules. It will take some major convincing to get her to accept her fate. What concerns me more is what has yet to come. Dolberg are cousins with Fagan Pack. Their mate, Dani, now assists with investigations into criminal activity amongst were. They'll find out that Melena is the daughter of Zeikele Mahalan. That will place Melena in more danger than anything we could protect her from alone."

"Looks like we'd better prepare ourselves best we can for the invasion of Dolberg Pack."

Chapter 8

"Who is this woman, that no one on my team can find her?" Count Divanni asked as his main guards gathered around him.

"We have looked everywhere. We have people watching the offices at the city council building downtown," Colin told Divanni.

"I don't understand it. She's human. She is weak."

"She's working for Xavier Dolberg. His nephews are searching for her, too."

"What? Why?"

"Not quite sure. My sources believe that she is of importance to the city council because of some special project she has been working on. I am trying to get more information without making it obvious."

Divanni rubbed his chin and stared off toward the window.

"A special project, you say? I wonder if this has anything to do with Kordosky?"

"Um, that's another thing sir. The last person seen with the woman was the vamp," Wilton, one of his guards, informed him.

"Damn. How does a human know a vampire like Kordosky? He is a loner, a bloodletter that avoids any type of relationship, business or otherwise."

"Maybe Togar Filletto may know. It seems that Lance had taken a liking to the blonde as well," Wilton said.

Divanni felt his hackles rise. "Filletto has Zera. There is no way he would give up an Alpha female for a human female. No matter how well-endowed the blonde is. Lance is the one to watch out for. It may have seemed that he was interested in the blonde for his boss, but you know Lance's tastes are a bit on the extreme side. The blonde wouldn't survive the torture. I want you all to discreetly watch the city council building, Xavier Dolberg, and his nephews. If you can track Kordosky, then follow him, too. One of these men will lead us to her and we will be able to find out exactly who she is. In the interim, Wilton, you have a job to do. Everyone else, go and find this woman."

The room cleared out, leaving Wilton and Divanni.

"Wilton, I need you to get in touch with Mercer Collette. Lay on the pressure and get that wolf to submit to giving up information on this secret operation taking place with the city council. I need to make sure that Xavier Dolberg, his nephews, and Fagan Pack are not onto our little exploratory operation. We cannot have were investigators catching wind of this operation. If Samantha or Lord Crespin, never mind anyone associated with the circle of elders, catches on to my near discovery, then we could lose everything I have been working to achieve. I will not head to the islands to dig with these wolves or vampires over my shoulders. This is mine. I am meant to rule and pick the new members of the circle of elders. We could have lost even more when they discovered the warehouse and the documents that were there."

"Sir, I will take care of it. My men are already stationed secretly amongst the city council building, in the town where Samantha and Lord Crespin reside as well as in the department that Dani and Fagan Pack work out of. If there is anything that even remotely indicates that they are onto you, I will be made aware of it as well as Colin. Also, I tried to confiscate the silver knife that was used by the woman to kill Phillip. Dolberg Pack beat me to it. I did get a picture of it on my cell phone."

Wilton passed over his phone to the count.

"That looks like part of the set that was stolen from the warehouse office. How could this woman possess it?"

"Are you sure, sir?"

"Not a hundred percent. It doesn't make any sense. The questions about this woman are growing. Find her, so we can move on with the plan."

"I'll let you know when things seem secure."

"Excellent. If this location is correct, I will hold the Book of Founding Fathers in my hands and truly prove once and for all that Divanni was amongst the first leaders of the circle of elders. Add in the bonus of the jewels, and no man, or wolf would ever have enough money or power to defeat me."

Chapter 9

"It would be wise to come back to work so we can discuss what happened the other night, Melena," Xavier Dolberg said as he leaned back in his chair by his desk.

"I'm sorry, Xavier, but the other night scared me. There were men shifting, a vampire tried to take me back to his estate, another man tried to bite me, so I stuck him with a silver knife and five huge men were after me as well. I believe they were your nephews."

"I heard about the wolf who attempted to mark you. He was one of Filletto's men. In regards to the vampire, I will speak with Julius today. Now, my nephews are a completely different story. They would not bring any harm to you, Melena. In fact, they would protect you like no one else."

He heard her snort of disbelief.

"I doubt that. I may not be a wolf, but I do know how you men, especially, operate. It was a mistake to attend the event. I prefer to remain in the background, doing the research and investigative stuff. I want to do the job that you hired me to do and to just be left alone. I prefer it this way."

"You have done amazing work for the city. I need you by my side to continue developing the project. It's crucial that we have the right people involved and it seems you have a knack for choosing them. Despite the scare that Julius caused, he hadn't actually harmed you in any way, am I correct?"

"I supposed him licking my neck and trying to enter my mind isn't too harmful."

"You stopped him from doing it."

"How do you know that?"

"Because, if you hadn't and if Julius really wanted to feast on you, you would still be with him in his bed right now."

"My God, you wolves and vampires are awfully cocky. I did escape from him."

"He could have caught you just as easily. That doesn't matter. I know Julius well. He is a good person to have on our side. Now, will you please come back to work? I need your help."

He heard her sigh and he hoped that he was convincing her to come back. He already spoke to his nephews and staff about providing extra security for her. He couldn't believe that the address she gave as her place of residence was false. He should be greatly concerned that she was one of the bad guys, yet every instinct both were and man, told him she was trustworthy and to allow the events to unfold.

"I am used to being alone and handling things on my own. I prefer my privacy and I don't want a bunch of were men sniffing around, trying to choose me for their entertainment. I've heard the stories."

He cleared his throat. "I can assure you that you will be left alone to do your job. We have so much to do. This group needs to be tight, organized, and trustworthy. I need your help, Melena. I wouldn't even trust someone else to take this over or even enter your system of organization."

She chuckled. She was an organized mess. One look in her office and he wondered how the hell she even knew where anything was.

"I will try to come by, but please ensure that I am not bothered. There are things that need to be done before finalizing the fifth choice."

"I understand. Be safe and call me if you need anything at all."

Xavier hung up the phone and stared at his nephew Gideon.

Gideon stood with his arms crossed in front of his chest and his teeth clenched.

"She's hiding something, Uncle. I can't believe that Julius licked her."

Xavier leaned forward, placed his hands on his desk and stood up.

"I'm afraid that she is hiding something, too. But I still feel that she can be trusted. Whatever she is hiding must be personal to keep her alone and so weary of relationships and trust. Julius's interest in her and the fact that he didn't just take what he wanted says an awful lot. Too much if you ask me."

"I agree. He was quite cryptic the last time I spoke with him. If you do not trust her to confide in you, then how come you have her working on something so crucial to our safety as were and the safety of the circle of elders?" Gideon asked.

"She can be trusted. I know this. My gut is insistent that she is important to this development and that any reservations or distrust she has is personal. Her personal life was not even important to me until you and your brothers told me that you believe her to be your mate. It was all business, but if she is going to be family, then she will need to learn to trust each of us."

"My gut is tied up in knots and I don't feel too confident in the gods' choice. She has gained the interest of my enemies. Our enemies, and because she is more human than were, she could be persuaded the wrong way."

"Then it's our job to ensure that she gets all the right information and that we keep her out of the hands of the enemy. Eventually she will come around."

"Unfortunately, Uncle, that is going to be utter hell and torture for me and my brothers. Our wolves need to claim her and secure her beside us. Being that we are not so tamed, for lack of a better word, we could scare the crap out of her. Right now my skin is crawling, just egging my wolf to shift and howl for the simple fact that she was on the phone with you and I could hear her voice. My wolf knows that she is mine. My brothers and I already lost one mate. We will not lose Melena."

"You will need to control those urges. She is, as you say, more human than were. I think the best thing to do is to see if Melena shows up for work. We need to make her feel safe."

"Agreed. But one of us will be here to speak with her. She will need to learn about us, as men, as wolves, and as her mates."

* * * *

"So what do you think these letters stand for?" Melena asked Saxton and Tango as they looked over the pictures of the documents she confiscated from the warehouse.

"I never heard of anything called TAMW. Perhaps it's an acronym for something," Saxton said.

"Maybe we should Google search it or Bing it? That is bound to give us something," Tango said.

"Not if it's a secret code for some kind of group or operation. Aren't either of your wolf senses picking up on anything?" Melena asked with a bit of sarcasm.

"What's with the wolf senses comment?" Saxon asked.

"Nothing. I'm just frustrated. I mean, let's say that I do have some were blood in me. Why can't I pull from that power and use it? If I could come in tune to my inner wolf senses, then I could have smelled what packs were at that warehouse or even recognized more things."

"It's not like that, Melena. This is not like a fiction novel. There is much more to our capabilities as wolves," Saxton said.

"Yeah, there's this inner power and sensation that goes beyond gut instincts. Acknowledging those sensations and emotions places one in tune to their wolf. You have great natural instincts," Tango told her.

"Yeah, but not like a wolf does. Perhaps if you two would share more facts about my life and identity, it could help clear up some confusion here?"

"Hey, look at this picture. Do you see that, Saxton?" Tango asked, conveniently changing the subject, as he pointed to the picture of a desk with papers and business cards on it. To the side was a handwritten note with a symbol.

Saxton looked at it and growled low.

"What? What is it?" Melena asked.

"That's Donovan Kylton's business symbol for his chain of banks," Saxton replied.

"Donovan is a member of the circle. I saw him at the event the other night. He was very friendly with the Dolberg men and spoke with Count Divanni."

"This could be the clue we've been waiting for. I'd hate to think someone in the circle, a man like Donovan, would be assisting the enemy. But what else can we assume from this picture? He was there at the warehouse. He could be the one informing the count of any updates in security," Saxton stated.

"Or it could be an associate," Tango added.

"He is friends with Xavier and he is the one, the fifth choice to become a member of the Security Ring," Melena said then looked angry.

"Holy shit," Tango added.

"I'm going to have to go to work. I need my resources there to investigate Donovan fully as well as his employees."

"That is not a good idea. Others could be looking for you still," Tango said.

"I guess it's time for another great disguise, Saxton."

* * * *

It was late in the evening when Melena snuck in through the side entrance to the building. She knew that Xavier was still upstairs in his office working, but she wanted to filter through the old files in the basement, where she could get information on Donovan and his department. With their identification numbers she could research them on a secure network.

She was looking over the files when she thought she heard a noise. Just as she turned around, she caught sight of the two men standing there with arms crossed in front of their massive chests.

She nearly gasped at the sight of them. Dark blue eyes, jet-black hair, Gideon and Edric Dolberg were gorgeous. Better looking than the old picture Saxton and Tango had shown her.

"Breaking and entering is a crime, sweetheart." Gideon looked her over. Talk about intimidation? These men projected it like nothing else she ever experienced before. She felt her heart rate increase. She felt her body react immediately in a positive way. This was insane. She held in her reaction, kept a straight face and willed herself to be cool and in control.

Edric slowly took a step toward her.

She placed the open filing drawer between herself and him.

"I work here, so it's not breaking and entering. How about you two?" She turned toward the filing cabinet and pushed the file she was looking on back down. She ran her hands over all of the files in case these wolves decided to sniff where she had been. She wouldn't want them to catch onto her investigation.

She closed up the cabinet and stared at them.

Edric reached toward her and she feared his touch as he flipped a strand of the long strawberry-red hair.

"A redhead now? What's with all the disguises?" Edric asked, looking down at her.

She didn't like the feelings she was getting. Her body felt aroused. Her nipples hardened. What was it about these men that made her react like this? She needed to get upstairs. She shouldn't be alone with men this big and powerful.

"Sorry, buddy, but the interrogation tactics don't apply to us humans. If you'll excuse me." She started to walk away when she felt the large hand gently grasp her fingers.

"Wait. Don't run off again. We want to talk with you."

Oh God, he has huge fingers and hands. She immediately felt so feminine and petite compared to them. Why was she attracted to such obviously wild men?

"There's nothing to talk about. I don't know either of you."

"Get to know us then," Gideon stated, and she turned immediately toward him and his commanding tone.

It wasn't a casual invite. No way. It was laced with command and order. *He's ordering me to get to know him. Pompous wolf.*

He looked her over and she felt like moaning from the warm sensations that flowed through her. Melena wondered if wolves had similar powers like vampires? Could they control her somehow through mind control?

"I need to head upstairs to speak with Xavier. Please, just leave me alone."

She started toward the door when she felt the hand on her waist. Abruptly she pulled from the contact and hit the wall behind her.

Both men's eyes widened in shock at her reaction.

"Don't touch me. Stay clear of me," she stuttered as she pointed at them, while taking a few steps backward before she hurried out of the room and up the stairs.

Before she could reach the door, Xavier was pulling it open.

"Melena, thank goodness you're okay. I was getting worried when you hadn't shown up earlier today."

"I'm sorry, Xavier. I thought it was safe to come here and get some work done."

Just then Gideon and Edric entered the hallway.

"You've met my nephews, correct?"

"Yes. I need to speak with you. Alone," she stated, and Xavier looked at his nephews.

"We'll talk later, Melena," Gideon said, and she felt the chills run over her body. She watched as both men left and then she walked into Xavier's office.

"So what is going on?" Xavier asked and she began to explain her findings.

"This can't be true. Not Donovan. It must be a mistake."

"That is why I showed up here tonight. I wanted to get a hold of the old files downstairs but I noticed there are some pages of information missing. Why is that?"

"There shouldn't be anything missing from those files. They came directly from the government. Lance Collette was in charge of securing those files years ago."

"Well something is missing in them. In regards to the employees Donovan has working in the New York location of Wolf Bay Banks."

"What are you thinking?"

"I'm thinking that if Donovan himself isn't in cahoots with Filletto and the count, then perhaps one of his employees is. I have a list and I want to investigate each of them."

"Well then it's good that Gideon and Edric are here. They can assist you. They've known Donovan Kylton for years."

"No. I do not want anyone helping me. I work better alone."

Xavier stared at her.

"They will not hurt you, Melena. In fact, if there is something criminal going on around the circle, then these men can be of assistance."

She swallowed hard.

"I work alone, Xavier. I had hoped to make the decision of choosing Donovan as a member of the Security Ring. I hate to think that my judgment was so far off and that I could have jeopardized everything you and the others have been working for."

"Nonsense, Melena. You have been key in creating this organization of security. Yes, it has taken some time and will continue to take time, but it must be done. I'll tell you what? The Dolberg Pack is at your disposal. If you need them to assist, then they will comply."

"I won't need them," she replied confidently then exited the office. A glance over her shoulder and she saw both Gideon and Edric watching her before they entered their uncle's office.

* * * *

It had been two hours since she started researching the list in hand.

She wasn't coming up with much. But then she found out that one of Donovan's employees from the New York branch here in the city was related to Valdamar Pack. That particular wolf pack was huge in the were hierarchy.

Her head was beginning to hurt, and as she glanced at the clock, she saw that it was nearly two in the morning. She closed off the computer, locked up her notes, and grabbed her backpack.

Dressed casually in dress pants, low-heeled shoes, and a blouse, she headed out of the office. Xavier's lights were off, indicating that he had left for the evening. As she exited the building, she headed toward the bus stop when she thought she heard some noises. Glancing around, she had the funny feeling that someone was watching her. That was when she caught sight of one man about twenty feet in front of her. A car skidded to a halt by the curb in front of the bus stop and she knew that she was in danger.

As she turned to walk in the other direction and perhaps run, she nearly slammed into another man. He grabbed her by her shoulders and she ducked and stepped back.

"Whoa, sweetheart, don't be afraid. We just want to talk to you."

"I don't know you."

"No, you don't, but we need to take you to someone who does want to know you. Come on." He reached his hand out and she stepped back.

"I don't think so."

"Oh come on, sweetheart. He'll make it worth your while. You'll never want to leave him."

As she turned to run, the other two men were there. She sidestepped, unsure where to go, when one of the other guys reached for her arm. A quick turn and she pulled from his grasp just as the deep, loud voices approached.

"I don't think the young lady wants you to touch her."

She was surprised to see Gideon, Edric, and Chordeo, but as the feeling of relief hit her, the situation got out of control.

The one guy who spoke to her first grabbed her around the waist and hoisted her up over his shoulder. She struggled to get free, realizing just how strong these were men were.

She could hear some grunts and growling as the one guy tried to toss her into the backseat of the car. She kicked him hard in the groin and scooted backward across the seat to the other door. She opened it and fell onto the ground, before jumping up.

As she turned to run, there was another guy she didn't recognize.

He reached for her and she swung her forearm at his throat as he bent to grab her.

He grunted and she ran, right into Saxton and Tango. Tango took the guy out with one punch then stared at the bodies lying on the ground.

Gideon was yelling at one of the guys and questioning him.

"Are you okay?" Saxton asked as he held her.

"Yes. What the hell was that all about? Who are they?"

"Divanni's men," Saxton said.

"Release her now."

Melena turned around to see Gideon Dolberg.

His eyes were slightly glowing and one glance up toward Saxton and both he and Tango appeared on the defensive, too, as they showed their wolf eyes.

"They're with me," she stated toward Gideon, and he didn't look pleased. She shouldn't have even cared but instead she felt guilty for some odd reason.

"Let's get her out of here." Saxton remained holding her as he and Tango escorted her away from the scene. She wasn't surprised to find Gideon and Edric following. They hadn't walked far when she heard Gideon's voice right behind her.

"Where are you taking her?"

"Out of here," Tango stated firmly then placed himself between her and Gideon. Edric growled.

Saxton put his hand up.

"We are not the enemy."

"That is yet to be confirmed," Gideon replied.

"They aren't," Melena added.

Saxton grabbed her hand and pulled her closer to him.

"We need to get her out of here."

A large black SUV pulled up and the door opened.

"Need a lift?"

She recognized Chance immediately. He had a sparkle in his blue eyes and a bit of jokester in him.

As Saxton went to say something in response, a large dark-colored van with tinted windows approached and men got out and began to arrest the men the Dolberg men had restrained.

"Let's go," Gideon stated firmly in that very commanding tone and they all got into the SUV.

Melena was going to sit between Saxton and Tango but there was just enough room in the SUV for the five Alpha Dolberg wolves and Saxton and Tango. She maneuvered onto Saxton's lap and the entire cabin filled up in low growls. Saxton smirked as he held Gideon's gaze and Tango chuckled then placed his hand on Melena's knee.

Something told her that the Dolberg men were jealous. The thought made her belly quiver as she glanced at three of the five Alphas. Chordeo and another brother she hadn't met, and had to be

Mano, were in the front seat. Gideon, Chance, and Edric were much larger than Saxton and Tango and they were six feet tall. The SUV went over a bump and she grabbed onto Saxton. Another set of low growls moved through the cabin.

"How about you come on over here, honey, and sit on my lap?" Chance said in a very sexy and powerful manner. She immediately felt her body react to his tone and the deep blue of his eyes as they held her gaze. Man, could she get lost in his eyes.

She shook her head.

"She's fine where she is. Where are we going?" Tango asked.

"What do you want with Melena?" Saxton asked.

"We want to talk to her," Gideon replied and she could tell this was some kind of wolf pissing contest. But in the enclosed space, she could practically feel the testosterone and need to fight.

"Talk to her about what? She doesn't work for you. She works for your uncle," Saxton replied.

"It's more of a personal nature," Gideon said and she stared at him. His face was so intense looking right now. He kept his very large hands on his knees, and she could see the muscles in his forearms. He appeared to be built from solid rock. He was so close she could reach out and trace the hard lines of his jaw with her fingertip. There was no doubt in Melena's mind that Gideon was a force to reckon with.

"Personal? I don't think so. I don't even know you," she replied with attitude and his one eyebrow raised a bit as if he wasn't used to people talking back to him or perhaps a woman doing it. That annoyed her as she held his gaze. She had never been surrounded by such charismatic, attractive, and sexy men in her entire life. The fact that she felt somewhat like Thumbelina really twisted her thoughts.

"I can ensure you that if you give my brothers and I a bit of time we can explain things so that you understand."

His cocky, sure-fire attitude unnerved her. So in response, she did what came naturally and went on the defensive. She wasn't easily intimidated. She stared right back at him. Willed her eyes to roam over his body as if it didn't affect her one bit at all.

"Explain what? I don't know any of you and this is a waste of time. I have work to do. You should let us out on the next corner."

"No. You are our mate. You're not leaving our sight," Edric said, causing her heart to race as she shifted on Saxton's lap.

She swung her head toward him and glared.

Now Edric was getting all bossy and controlling, too. If all five of these men were like this, she surely would lose her mind with frustration. She now stared at him and looked him over as if that sensational body of his was available on every street corner or even on shelves nationwide.

"I do not belong to anyone. I don't know about this mate thing or whatever you are talking about, but I'm not interested."

Edric held her gaze and leaned forward. In the small confines of the space, his knee now touched hers.

"You don't know what you're saying. We'll explain it to you when we get to our place."

"I'm not interested and I am not a wolf. Back off."

Edric smirked then leaned back but not before squeezing her knee gently with his hand. She felt the sensation move up her body and straight to her pussy. This time the Dolberg men smirked and both Saxton and Tango growled low.

* * * *

It was a positive sign that Melena responded to Edric's touch in such a way. Every wolf in the vehicle smelled her arousal. Gideon had to fight the urge to take her into his arms and taste her for himself.

"Whose idea was it to cram into this vehicle with a mate we cannot touch?" Chance asked through their mind link.

"It seemed like a good idea at the time. I didn't know it would be like this. The urge, the need to have her and possess her is nearly overwhelming," Mano added from the front seat.

"What is her relationship with Saxton and Tango? Weren't they members of the Brothers of Were at one time about ten years ago?" Edric asked.

"Check into that with Dani and maybe Sam," Gideon said.

"Just get us to the estate and out of this vehicle," Edric said.

* * * *

Melena observed what she could about Gideon, Chordeo, and Edric. The three of the five brothers were just about identical. They shared the same black hair and blue eyes. Edric seemed easygoing, yet determined and in charge. It could be the whole Alpha thing, but the others were more obvious about it. Chordeo was intense. Even the way his eyes zeroed in on her body, made her feel alive, and on edge, but Gideon took the cake. The man had such a hard, unapproachable persona that it actually made her nervous. Whenever she got nervous, she gained attitude. She had a feeling that her mouth might get her into a heap of trouble.

She caught Chordeo's gaze and couldn't help but find his physical appearance attractive. Big muscles, tattoos on his arms and neck. The man looked lethal. Finally the SUV came to a stop. Melena went to climb out of the SUV but Edric lifted her into his arms then slowly slid her body down his as he held her.

"I wouldn't want you to fall," he said, and she swallowed hard. The man was big and filled with muscles. As her body moved down his, she felt the stone beneath her breasts. This was insane.

As she pulled away, Saxton guided her toward the estate and she was pleasantly surprised to see the gated entryway. They were about thirty minutes outside of the main city. As they entered the small building, she noticed that there weren't any personal items tossed about. In fact, it looked rather cold and un-lived-in.

"Can we get you something to drink?" Chordeo asked her.

She shook her head.

"I'm Mano." The one she hadn't met, but knew of him from the photograph she pulled from files, greeted her. He was exceptionally handsome. She found herself staring at him and his gorgeous blue eyes. What had Saxton and Tango said about the were men not being like the men described in romance novels? Oh, how wrong they were. Men shouldn't have such sexual appeal. She wondered what Mano might look like naked. These types of thoughts were going to get her in over her head.

She didn't bother to speak. She just nodded her head as he inhaled as if gathering her scent.

She felt a combination of oddness and interest. When she saw his eyes glow as he inhaled, she squinted her eyes to see if it were real. He turned away.

"Would you like to sit down?" Chance asked this time.

She glanced toward Chance. Surrounded by such gods and maintaining a blasé reaction was difficult to say the least.

"I would like for you to get on with what it is you need to talk about. We have things to do and it's late," she stated.

They all stared at her with such intensity. She felt something very deep inside of her. An almost overwhelming awareness of their strength and power. It should have pissed her off, made her feel like fighting them, but there were five of them. She didn't need someone to tell her that pissing these wolves off would be a mistake.

She sighed in annoyance then moved toward the set of couches, as if there really wasn't much of a choice. Her legs felt kind of wobbly. She felt unsteady with them staring at her. She sat down, crossed her legs, placed her hands clasped on her lap, and stared ahead at the bare marble fireplace. She didn't care what they told her. This was not their home. No home ever felt so cold and unlived in.

Behind her she could hear Gideon speaking with Saxton and Tango. Before she could turn around to see where they were headed, Edric, Mano, and Chance joined her. Mano took a seat on the ottoman in front of her legs. He scooted forward and she had to move her crossed legs to the right to make room for him. Their knees touched and she gasped at the electric shock she felt. Simultaneously, Chance took a seat on her right and Edric on her left.

The cushions sunk lower and every part of her body came alive. She swallowed hard as she held Mano's gaze. Her heart was racing, her palms were sweaty and her pussy felt as if it throbbed to be touched. With each breath she took, her breasts became sensitive and she closed her eyes and tried not to rub them.

"It's normal, Melena. Everything you're feeling is completely normal," Chance whispered, his mouth was inches from her ear. She popped her eyes open and stretched to the left only to bump into Edric's shoulder. He smiled at her.

"Please, just relax and let it happen."

She shook her head. No words could leave her lips. She was shocked at what they were doing to her. Her body must still be on edge after those men back there tried to take her. Who were they and who did they work for? Was it Filleto or the count?

Mano placed his hands over hers and she straightened her body as she tried to pull her hands from his. He didn't allow it as he smiled so sweetly it made her heart soar with appreciation for the man's fine looks and natural charm, never mind his strength.

Edric placed his hand on her thigh and she jumped.

"Easy, baby. We don't want to scare you."

She tried to speak, yet nothing came out. She swallowed, feeling her dry throat. This was so not like her. Stuck in a small, enclosed space with three wolf men with incredible, hot bodies and immense masculinity and she folded so easily?

"Please, you're scaring me. You're too much, too close. Please."

Chance placed his hand against her cheek and turned her toward him.

His hand was huge. She felt her body quiver. It was a mix of anticipation, excitement, and uncertainty.

She stared up into his dark, ocean-blue eyes and was mesmerized by the flecks of black and the emotion she saw. It made her pause in awe and gave him the opportunity he intended.

"I am going to kiss you. I've waited, but patience isn't possible with a woman as gorgeous and appealing as you."

His words sent a bolt of pride through her body and as his lips moved closer, his warm breath collided with her mouth and she breathed him in. Closing her eyes, something inside her accepted him and then his lips touched hers.

It was their first kiss and she memorized everything about it. Chance was filled with muscles, even along his jaw, neck, and shoulders, yet his lips were not hard and cold. They were somewhere between soft and firm, commanding and experienced.

When his tongue pressed through her parted teeth, deepening the casual kiss into a more sexual one, she reached up and placed her hand over his much larger hand.

It was then that the reality of his size, their sizes, intimidated her.

Chance must have felt her begin to pull away because he deepened the kiss, projecting his dominance, and then slowly released her lips as he cupped her face between his hands.

"Hot damn, woman, you taste amazing."

"I can't wait to take a taste, too."

It was then that she remembered the audience. Her cheeks warmed as she lowered her eyes and cleared her throat.

"I want to go." She stood up. She nearly lost her balance but Mano stood with her and placed his hands on her waist. This close, toe to toe, she stared up, with her head nearly tilted back to her shoulders and was in awe.

"Holy crap, you're big."

He smiled and she felt the palms of his hands cup her backside and pull her against him.

Their bodies collided. She inhaled a sharp breath.

Her pussy leaked and she tightened her thighs.

She pressed her hands against his chest and was shocked at the feel of steel beneath her fingertips. He was hard, solid, and very good-looking. His hair was not as short as Chance's and Edric's. Nor was it as long as Gideon's. He also had a look in his eyes that made her feminine instincts kick in. Mano was a charmer.

She tried to step back and he used one hand to keep her in place and against him, and the other slowly, gently moved up her hip, her arm and to her head, leaving goose bumps along the path.

He tilted her face up toward him, his hands huge against her skin.

"One kiss, to hold me over."

She felt her throat tighten up. My God, these men were outrageous. How the hell could any sane woman keep them at bay? Even the most experienced woman would find resisting them impossible. She wasn't experienced. She was a virgin and a bookworm when it came to imagining love stories and sexual encounters. Her heart raced and she felt the need to bolt and then Edric placed his hands on her hips from behind as Mano kissed her softly on the lips. The dual touch and feeling of being surrounded by such large, sexually powerful men shocked her. She was lost in Mano's kiss, in Edric's caresses along her hips and then up her ribs. As Edric's fingers grazed just below the swell of her breasts, Mano plunged his tongue deep within her mouth and devoured her moans.

Melena was overwhelmed with sensations and emotions. Her breasts tingled and her mind chanted for Edric to touch her breasts, fondle them, and do something to them. She was shocked and stopped herself from making a huge mistake. Both men sensed her pulling away and Mano eased his mouth from hers, kissing her lips, then her cheeks before smiling down at her. Edric squeezed her back against his chest and whispered against her cheek.

"You smell incredible. I can't wait to taste you, mate." His warm lips touched her cheeks and mouth as the realization of his statement hit her hard. *Mate? Taste me?*

She pulled from them, wiped away their kisses with the sleeve of her blouse, then clenched her teeth.

* * * *

"Who is she really?" Gideon asked Saxton and Tango. His brother Chordeo stood by the open doorway with his arms crossed in front of his massive chest.

Saxton knew that he and his friend Tango were big men and big wolves, but they were almost dwarves compared to Dolberg Pack. Now two of the largest, Gideon and Chordeo, stood before them.

"I'm sorry, Gideon, but her true identity must remain hidden. It is what the gods have determined."

Gideon released a long sigh. His dark eyes squinted and he appeared angry. Saxton's wolf was on guard. He didn't want to fight him or his brothers. He needed to buy Melena some time.

He looked toward the doorway. His concern over Melena being alone with Dolberg Pack brothers was obvious.

"She is our mate. We will protect her. There is no need for your concern."

"You're wrong, Gideon. Melena does not want to accept you or your brothers as her mates."

Gideon crossed his arms and stood in a confident stance. He appeared smug.

"She doesn't have a choice. It is her destiny," Gideon replied.

"She is our destiny," Chordeo added.

Saxton glanced at Tango and Tango widened his eyes but appeared as if their fight was useless.

"I can only tell you a little bit for now, Gideon. Her safety is mine and Tango's priority. Filletto, the count, and Coriano Morago must not get their hands on her. If they realize who her family is and what bloodline she is from, it could mean the beginning to an end for were law as we know it."

Gideon uncrossed his arms and stared at Saxton. "We are part of a special organization besides SWAT Team Seven."

"We know. As I am sure you recall, Tango and I were part of the Secret Order at one time."

"What changed that?" Chordeo asked, and he sounded both disappointed and distrusting.

"Melena happened. We were asked to step down from our positions and provide protection for Melena and training. We have been doing that for over a decade."

"Who is she?" Gideon asked again.

Saxton stared at him.

"I cannot tell you right now."

"You know she is our mate. There is nothing you can do to stop us from marking her and completing the mating bond," he stated firmly.

"Our brothers are helping to ease her fear right now," Chordeo said with confidence.

Saxton looked at Tango who started to head toward the doorway. Gideon and Chordeo stood in his path.

"We need to know who she is so we can protect her as you two have. We confiscated the knife she used to defend herself against Phillip. We can get prints off of that and run them," Gideon stated.

Saxton felt his gut clench.

"You won't want to do that. You will regret letting her identity go public too soon. I beg of you to trust us," Saxton said.

"Trust you? When you obviously don't even trust the fact that we are her intended mates?" Chordeo added.

"It won't matter if she is killed. You disclosing her identity will cause that," Tango added.

Saxton held Gideon's gaze. The wolf was smart and he would follow his gut.

"We will give you space but we need to keep in contact with her. She is ours and now that our wolves know that our mate exists, we will need her by our side sooner than later."

"Understood, Gideon. I will give you all our contact information. Let us finish doing the job we were asked to do. But also know that Melena is quite stubborn."

"I am certain we can handle our mate," Gideon replied.

"We'll soon see, Gideon. It's time for us to leave and Melena is coming with us."

Gideon allowed them to exit the room first with Chordeo leading the way back to the living room.

* * * *

"Stay away from me. I will not be controlled, manipulated, or used by wolves. Never."

"Melena?"

The sound of Saxton's voiced filled the room. She turned and he was there, taking her hand, and pulling her close to him. Edric, Mano, and Chance growled low.

"Easy, brothers. He is not a threat," Gideon said then joined them in the small confines of the living room.

"I want to leave. Right now," Melena said.

"We will. We'll explain everything tonight," Saxton said.

"She's leaving?" Edric asked, sounding disappointed. Melena felt the tinge of guilt then reminded herself that she wasn't a possession. She had a job, an agenda, and these men were not going to control her and keep her as their prisoner.

"They have work to do and things to discuss with Melena. We'll meet up tomorrow," Gideon said as Saxton and Tango nodded their heads toward Gideon.

She stared at Gideon, the obvious leader of this group of Alpha wolves. He was definitely leader material in every aspect of the word.

He also looked kind of untamed with his wavy hair and constant serious expression. The other wolves she had met over the years showed similar facial expressions of arrogance and superiority. Gideon, however, made it seem natural and respectable. She also hadn't had a reaction to any other wolves in the way she did with Gideon and his brothers. When Gideon stared at her, she felt a tingling sensation travel through her body. It was almost as if she felt him trying to read her mind or learn her, by observation.

She stared right back at him until Saxton took her hand. "Melena, we should go."

Melena, Saxton, and Tango began to walk from the house. As they exited and headed down the driveway past the SUV, she wondered why they weren't driving them back, then realized that Saxton and Tango still wanted their safe house to remain unknown.

In the back of her mind she thought about Julius. As a warm sensation traveled from her wrist and along the skin of her upper arm, she pulled it against her chest and glanced around the darkness. *Is he here? Is he watching me?*

She looked over her shoulder at the Dolberg brothers. The small army of massive men lifted their chins into the air then appeared menacing and uptight. She looked to Saxton and Tango for answers but Saxton gave her hand a small tug and pulled her along the pathway and down the street.

She knew that Julius was there. But why?

Chapter 10

Saxton wanted to come clean. He wanted to explain who her father really was and his importance to the circle and to all were. He felt guilty at the moment because he and Tango had in fact lied to her. As Brothers of Were, they pledged eternal loyalty to the circle, the were authority, and all its members, and they pledged an allegiance to their continued leadership and control. The circle ensured that every were respected the laws of the Founding Fathers. Through his connections to the circle, he became aware recently of individuals who were abusing their power to better themselves and not the were community overall. Too many children and future leaders were becoming casualties of unnecessary battles. But more recently, he received information an hour ago about the Morago organization. Coriano Morago recently purchased a large parcel of land near Waikiki, Hawaii. It included land surrounding Melena's family estate that was left behind when she fled. It hadn't been for sale. Saxton was told by higher-ups that the land would be maintained and kept for Melena's hopeful return one day.

Warnerbe Pierce was supposed to be one of the good guys, but apparently, he wasn't. Saxton placed Warnerbe in charge of safeguarding that land years ago. It appeared as if greed altered Warnerbe's loyalty to Saxton and Tango.

Saxton's cell phone rang and as he looked at the display screen he nearly gasped.

"Hello?"

"Hello, Saxton," Samantha said, and he smiled.

"How is the family?"

"Very well, thank you. And you? How are Tango and Melena?"

He leaned back into his chair and released a sigh.

"Taking in the fact that you just called me out of the blue, I am certain you have some idea about what is happening."

She chuckled. "You know me so well, Saxton. I understand that Melena is becoming restless. Her determination to develop a true Security Ring around the circle is commendable."

"You don't sound as enthusiastic as you were three years ago, Sam."

"Ah, three years ago I was new at this position of mine. The more information that is revealed to me the more chaotic my life becomes. You've done such a great job with Melena. My grandfather told me of her struggles and how her family was murdered. You and Tango have protected her thus far."

"Thus far? It sounds like she may be in danger."

"Oh, you know I cannot give up too much information. However, you do know how I operate. If I can be of any assistance, please don't hesitate to contact me. Or perhaps Dani. She and your cousins could be quite helpful."

"Now this is sounding interesting. So there is definitely something illegal going on with the count?"

"I didn't say a word. But, what else has been happening?"

He told Sam about the party Melena attended and about the Dolberg brothers and about Julius.

"My goodness, this is way more than what I expected. Have they mated yet? The five wolves and the vampire?"

"What? You think that Julius is her mate as well?"

Sam chuckled. "Don't freak out, Saxton. These things do happen. Look at Dani and Vanderlan. It happens and usually for a reason. Melena is special. That is why her father protected her and trained her the way he did. Zeikele had a feeling that someone might come to destroy him and his family because of his knowledge."

"What was it that Zeikele had knowledge of that Morago didn't want exposed?" Saxton asked.

"I believe it had something to do with some sort of were treasure. Unfortunately I do not know any more than you do. It is that secretive. It could be the Book of the Founding Fathers. All I can tell you is that Melena needs protection. If the gods have chosen Julius and Dolberg Pack, then it is going to get intense before it calms. I spoke with someone with insight. They believe Melena to be the one we have all been searching for to ensure the protection and sanctity of the circle. If this is true, then she holds the power within her to find a way to clean out those who do not belong as members and to rebuild the circle along with myself, Dani, and Ava."

"Holy crap. Why should I even let her out of my sight then? Why expose her to someone like Morago, Divanni, or Filletto getting their hands on her? I mean when Morago finds out that Zeikele's daughter survived the massacre, then what?"

"She will need Julius and Dolberg Pack. They know from experience what it is like to lose someone close to them. They also have seen firsthand the destruction and lack of empathy of life, as Melena experienced herself. All of the changes that have been occurring over the last decade have been for this. She needs to succeed in making the necessary changes and weed out the bad ones. Once her true identity is revealed, then many of our enemies will try to stop her from succeeding."

"Her true identity? You mean being Zeikele's daughter?"

"I mean being Goddess of the circle."

"Holy crap, Sam."

"Exactly, Saxton. I'm going to need to speak with Gideon and his brothers."

"I think you should hold off on that."

"Why?"

"Melena is not ready to face this aspect of her heritage as of yet," Saxton said rather sarcastically.

Sam chuckled. "Oh boy, what exactly have you and Tango been teaching her for the last ten years?"

"To be independent, to survive, and to fight for what she believes in."

"Don't forget about breaking into warehouses to secure family heirlooms and destroy rogue wolves doing illegal activities. Well then, once she realizes what having Alpha mates is all about, then she'll commit to them."

"Not when revenge is her sole focus. How did you know about the break-ins? Oh, forget I asked, I forgot that it was you, Princess, that I was speaking with. Her need for revenge is what concerns me most."

"Revenge?"

"On Morago. She will not rest until he is either broke or dead."

"I wouldn't worry so much about that, Saxton. You've taught her so much and you would be surprised how much the fates play a hand in our destinies. Be well and contact me if the need arises."

"Yes, Princess."

She chuckled and he disconnected the call. Samantha hated being called Princess, but that was who she was. A royal in the circle. *Now what am I going to do about Melena? I need to keep her safe and telling Dolberg may seem like a betrayal once Melena finds out. Then there's the whole mating thing. A vampire and five Alpha wolves? Melena is going to freak out about this.*

He heard someone clear their throat, and when he looked up, he saw Tango.

"Hey, what's going on?" Saxton asked as he leaned forward then stood up.

Tango stared at him.

"Did I hear that phone call correctly? Did Sam say Goddess of the circle?"

He should have been more careful. He knew that Melena was upstairs and getting ready, but Tango was a wolf, with excellent hearing.

"Close the door."

"Oh fuck." Tango closed the door and entered the office. He crossed his arms in front of his wide chest and gave Saxton a look of anger. Tango was a great friend. More like a brother really and their commitment to the Brothers of Were had been their sole purpose in life. When Zeikele had chosen them to be responsible for his family if anything had ever happened to him, they never expected Melena to be this special.

"What you heard is true. She is the Goddess. We should have known that Zeikele wouldn't leave us in charge of his only daughter unless she was of great importance."

"Of great importance? She is the one that many have been seeking to find," Tango said.

"More like seeking to destroy. If the stories are true, then Melena does have the capabilities to secure the circle for good. She possesses the instincts as her father did. She has already helped to establish the Security Ring."

"By being his daughter, the surviving child of Zeikele, she has a right to everything he once controlled and secured. She could be the leader of the Security Ring. This title could also secure her protection as far as the circle or other packs are concerned."

"No, it could make her a target. For abduction, threats, and manipulation. She does not understand or connect with her heritage yet. Plus, now she has the brooch. That is somehow key to that Book of the Founding Fathers," Saxton added.

"Perhaps after she is mated, her perspective on wolves and her heritage will change?"

"I think we should tell her. I think talking to her and explaining her family and now her role will make it easier for her," Tango said.

Saxton ran his fingers through his hair.

"We used to be threatening warriors. Now, here I am contemplating hurting the feelings of a child we raised.

"I hear your frustration, but she is not ours to keep, to mate, and to protect. She belongs in safekeeping. What could be better than five Alpha males known for their power, intimidation, and ability to secure?"

"One very powerful and selfish vampire," Saxton said then hit the intercom button on the desk.

"Melena, can you please meet Tango and I downstairs in the office now?"

He heard her response and released a sigh.

"Here it goes. She'll either love us or hate us," Saxton said.

* * * *

Melena was absolutely speechless. As Saxton and Tango filled her in on her father, his power and standing in the were world as she liked to refer to it, she felt ready to vomit. She was filled with a mix of emotions. There was anger, disgust, annoyance, but what really shocked her were the feelings of pride.

"So, you see, we had no choice. When you contacted us, we were told by your father to contact a close family friend to ensure your innocence and identity," Saxton said.

She stared at him, feeling the information overload but determined to understand everything he was saying.

"A family friend? What?"

"Basically, a goddess of magic. She shares your bloodline with others," Tango added.

"Wait. Are you saying that I still have family alive? I mean, I am totally trying to bypass the magic goddess thing for now, but family? Like Mahalan relatives?"

"Yes. They exist, but they, too, remain hidden."

"Why, Saxton?"

"Because they would be killed by the enemies who seek you out."

"Why am I so important? I don't even remember my childhood. How could I remember anything secretive that my father might have shared?"

"You've done a lot of research and seem to have a knack or instinct when researching were protocol and the allegiance to the circle. Ever hear of the Goddess of the circle?" Saxton asked. Tango rubbed his hand back and forth over his mouth. He was nervous and upset.

"Of course. The Goddess is believed to have the power to recreate the circle of elders or kind of like take out the trash and get rid of the bad members who are no longer loyal. If we could find her, then we could surely get rid of some of the bad members and replace them with the good ones who truly believe and respect were law. We might not even need the Security Ring, except as precaution and insurance."

They stared at her and she didn't understand why.

"Baby, you're her," Tango said when Saxton just stared at her.

"What?"

"You are the Goddess of the circle," Saxton whispered.

Melena thought she was going to fall off the chair. She felt her jaw drop. She closed her mouth and stared at them. Then her jaw dropped again.

"I...me?"

She stood up and began to pace the office.

"No way. No, you are mistaken. This can't be. I'm more human than were. You two said it."

"The magic spell that is over you helps to disguise your abilities and your scent."

She sniffed her shirt by pulling the material up to her nose.

"I smell like a goddess?"

"Wolves and other spiritual creatures could sense your unique scent. It is quite appealing and so incredible it draws all attention to you. They may not know exactly why they are so in tune to you, but they will be. That's why as the goddess, you would need to live in privacy and almost seclusion. By securing your identity, you can remain unknown yet get done what needs to be accomplished," Saxton said.

"I don't believe this. Yet, it makes total sense to me. When will the magic spell break? When will I gain any powers or insight into cleaning up the circle?"

"Whoa, Melena. There is much to go over. This power is a huge responsibility. If you were to fall into the wrong hands and be manipulated or led to believe certain things, then you could ultimately destroy centuries of were law and regulations. It could mean the end to any formal order and allow for anarchy and rogue wolves to attempt a takeover," Tango told her.

"Holy shit!" She plopped down onto the chair.

"There is a lot to go over, but we will provide as much information as possible."

"What about Gideon, Mano, Chordeo, Chance, and Edric? Is it true? Am I supposed to accept them as my mates? Will this ensure the protection of the circle?"

Saxton looked at Tango and released a sigh that seemed to be laced with unhappiness.

"They are your mates. They know it and they will protect you. Whether or not they will also protect the circle because of you, we will have to wait and see."

"I don't know if I can trust anyone else but you two." She felt the tears reach her eyes for the first time in so many years.

Then she sensed Tango and Saxton moving toward her. Saxton took her hand and Tango placed his hand on her shoulder. She looked up toward both of them.

"You will know what is right and what is wrong, by following your gut instincts. This is your destiny. To lead, to be strong, and to save the were community from destruction. The greed and criminal activity is running rampant in these times. We are losing so many good men and women to corruption and selfishness. Their use of were abilities and forcefulness must be controlled. The circle must once again be the ultimate decision maker," Saxton told her.

She stared at him with tears in her eyes as emotions and ideas filled her head.

"I'm glad I was paying attention to both of you over the years, as you explained in great detail about were law. Otherwise, I would be asking for a crash course right now that would add to the plethora of other emotions I am currently feeling. This is a lot to take in."

"It is, but you are more than capable of handling it. Plus, we intend to remain by your side even if we have to deal with your mates," Tango said and then gave her a wink.

"Then the Security Ring is a must. I have to help create this ring of true supporters. We have to figure out what that TAMW stands for."

Saxton and Tango smiled.

"You're going to be fine, Melena. You are an adult, a grown woman, and a goddess. The gods have chosen wisely." Tango pulled her into his arms and hugged her.

Melena had so many thoughts running through her head, but then came thoughts of her family. Members she never knew existed but needed to remain safe.

"Let's get down to business, guys. It's going to take some serious planning to bring down the bad guys."

Chapter 11

Julius watched Melena as she slept, just as he had done every night since finding out she was indeed alive. Except, he used his powers to keep her sleeping. He had made a mistake that first night. Allowing his desire to touch her and allowing her to see him, feel him so intimately had been wrong. He couldn't stop thinking about that night and wishing that somehow they could be together.

Sneaking in to see her, and to know that she was safe and resting helped ease his worry. It was his way of satisfying his need to be close to her, yet not jeopardize her happiness in any way. She was restless tonight, but as he tried to read her thoughts, he felt the magical block. His heart ached as his desire and hunger to have her was becoming more and more difficult to avoid.

Julius leaned down toward her face as he sat beside her on the bed. She was so beautiful in sleep. He could stare at her for hours and he did. He hadn't touched her since that first night and it was the most difficult thing he had ever done. He wondered now what she dreamt of and wished it was of him. He softly traced her chin and jaw then lowered his mouth toward hers. She was too delicious to resist tasting.

Even in sleep her body, her blood, and her soul pulled toward him. She kissed him back even though he controlled her in case she awoke. He didn't bother to change forms until it seemed she was coming out of her dream state. In a moment he shifted to air and used his mind to take just a little from her to ease the hunger.

Melena moaned as she open her thighs and thrust slowly upward.

You are so beautiful, goddess of mine. I long to be inside of you, connecting with you for eternity.

Melena awoke, once again shocking him.

She gasped then calmed her breathing.

"I know you're here, Julius. I feel you. Please show yourself. I need to see you."

He wrestled with his mind about revealing himself to her. How the hell did she know he was here?

He used his mind to unbutton the light nightshirt she wore. Her abundant breasts emerged beneath the fabric and he gasped in delight. She was fit for a king to feast upon.

"Just one taste. A small pleasure to ease my ache."

"Yes, Julius. Please, touch me, taste me. I want you to."

He licked across her nipple before pulling the tight bud between his sharp teeth. He circled it with his tongue then pulled hard. She moaned as she tilted her breasts upward toward his mouth.

"You're so responsive."

"You do this to me." She held his gaze.

He did the same to her other breast then cupped them with his hands. She was well endowed. He stared at her body, from breasts to belly. So badly he wanted more, but he had already gone too far. He had sworn that he wouldn't take a taste of her cream again. He couldn't. The more he thought of her the more he wanted. Slowly he straightened out her blouse, re-buttoned the top, then stared at her again. Her cheeks were flushed, her breathing slowly settled.

"Don't stop, Julius. Why did you stop?"

"I can't do this with you, Melena. As much as I want to, I made a promise. Sleep now," he told her then tried to use his powers to ease her mind. She lay back down and closed her eyes. He kissed her one last time before the sun came up.

* * * *

Melena opened her eyes, feeling the glare of the sun peek through the blinds. She thought she had closed them last night. She felt groggy and her breasts were tender. She cupped them with her hands, massaging the sensitive mounds as her mind tried to figure out why they ached. Immediately she thought of Julius and gasped. He was here last night. He watched her as she slept and he touched her, aroused her as she slept. She knew that it wasn't just a fantasy dream, but a reality. The vampire used his powers on her again to try and make her forget. But why? She told him that she wanted him to touch her. I like when he touches me, she admitted to herself. She immediately felt aroused and needed.

That thought made her think of the Dolberg Pack. Chance, Mano, Gideon, Edric, and Chordeo entered her mind. Goddamn, those men were sexy as damn hell. What it might feel like to have them touch her so intimately, like Julius had. She sighed in annoyance and now her body really felt strung tight and antsy.

"I'm horny. This is what my life has turned into. Danger around every corner, mystery and lies, sexual attraction to a crazy, somewhat insecure vampire and five, breathtakingly handsome, rugged, wild, Alpha were men with egos the size of Texas." She heard the knock on her door and jumped, being caught off guard.

"Yes."

"Can I come in?" It was Saxton.

She pulled the sheets around her and sat up on the side of the bed.

"Okay, come in."

"Hey, sorry to wake you, but I just heard from Gideon. He said that Mano, him, and Chance located the warehouse you had found weeks ago. It was cleared out, but they caught the scents of Filletto and Morago."

"Oh God. Morago is part of this, whatever it is."

"We should let them help us. Perhaps Dolberg will know what TAMW means."

"No. I need to do this and stay clear of them. I can't deal with this mating thing while trying to secure the sanctity of the circle. It's too much."

"They can help you. It could be why they were chosen for you as mates."

She released a long sigh.

"They have the silver knife in their possession. If they do the fingerprints analysis, which they may have already, matters could get worse. Plus, word is from my informants, Divanni has pictures of the knife. He could connect it to the warehouse and the fact that you are the one who stole the set."

"It was my father's set, not his."

He raised his eyebrows at her.

"We can use the wolves' help here. They're going to find out sooner or later that you are Zeikele's daughter."

"And the Goddess of the circle I suppose," she replied with attitude.

He shrugged his shoulders.

"Call them. Set up a location to meet."

"Okay. I'll tell them to meet us in an hour."

"We can meet them at the city council. That way we can inform Xavier of what is happening, too. Once we meet with Gideon and his brothers, we can have Xavier issue wolves to monitor Morago, Filletto, and Divanni."

"There's a chance that Divanni may be at the building today. They're doing a ribbon-cutting ceremony for the new park around the corner and the count made some financial contributions along with Filletto."

"That's typical, isn't it, Saxton? Bad guys trying to cover their illegal activities by showing face in the public eye."

"It's not your concern. You need to focus on developing the Security Ring. Tango, the Dolberg Pack, and I will work on monitoring the bad guys, as you like to call them. So hurry up and get ready. I'll make the call."

Saxton left the room and Melena took a deep breath then released it. She thought about Dolberg Pack. It was a shock that she actually felt the anticipation of seeing them again. This couldn't be good.

* * * *

"The woman, Melena Zekar, is working for Xavier Dolberg. A source inside the city council believes that she is part of a plan to organize security of some sort," Wilton told Divanni as he joined him in his office.

"How can that be? She is hardly even were. Why would Xavier or the council allow a human woman, no less, to be in charge of security of any sort?" Divanni asked.

"That is what I have people trying to find out. What I know so far is that she works alone, in the basement of the building and that she has full clearance. She had to have been the one who stole the set of knives. They belonged to the Mahalan collection."

"Full clearance? We could use her. Do you know to what extent her allegiance is to the circle and were law? If she can be bought or perhaps convinced to help me? This could be perfect. With her open access, she could keep us abreast of any investigations by the government or the circle and give us the heads-up in case our plan becomes exposed. Wow, Wilton. I am truly impressed with your capabilities. Where is she now? Perhaps she is not one of the good guys, but has gotten on the inside. Taking that set of knives has meaning. It has to. I need to find out what was taken, if anything, from the vault of money and antiques confiscated by the authorities at Dashkin and Lunvolk's place."

Wilton smiled. "I heard that the authorities found a person dressed in black escaping from the building as it was being raided on the surveillance cameras. It could have very well been this Melena, too. She is at the city council building. She arrived an hour ago with two other men. I am waiting to find out their identities and whom they work for."

"Excellent. I have to be there in twenty minutes. Bumping into her could be a great opportunity. Be sure to get pictures of the men who arrived with her. That way if they need to be eliminated, we can handle that simultaneously while I chitchat with the beauty. Wonderful work, Wilton. Keep me updated with anything new. Can you tell Tanner to get the car ready?"

"Yes, sir."

Wilton exited the room.

Divanni picked up his phone and called Morago. He explained about Melena.

"She can't be just some half blood, Divanni. She must be of importance or at least her family. Or perhaps she is working on her own to gain some power. I don't like it. How the hell could she sneak into a building and steal things while the SWAT teams raided the place? It's unbelievable. She has to have help."

"She doesn't have any family as far as we know right now. I think it would be smart and in our best interest to pick her up and question her."

"I think you're right. The last thing we need is some woman screwing up our plans of a takeover. When you get her, bring her to my place. I'll send a few men to assist you at the city council building."

Divanni hung up the phone then headed out the door. This could be the insurance he had hoped to have before digging for the treasure. This situation needed to be handled accordingly. He better tell Wilton to bring backup.

* * * *

"When is Melena supposed to get here?" Edric asked as he leaned back in the chair in the conference room. He and his brothers were dressed in SWAT attire, after spending the morning assisting in a drug raid. When they got the call from their uncle about meeting Melena, they hadn't had time to change.

"Any minute," Xavier said when they heard the knock at the door. Chance opened it and there stood Melena, Saxton, and Tango.

She looked incredible, as usual, but this time she wasn't in disguise.

She seemed to be taken aback by their attire. Her eyes widened and a small blush appeared on her cheeks.

"Good morning, gentleman. Shall we get started?" As she entered the room, wearing her knee-length, slim-fitting beige skirt and white blouse with a matching beige jacket, Edric and his brothers inhaled her scent. Edric felt his chest tighten and his cock harden instantly. She walked past Xavier carrying an attaché case and Gideon stopped her.

"No disguise today, sweetheart?" He ran his hand gently up her arm then back down again. She looked at his hand then back up at him.

"It's not necessary anymore. It's time to face the enemies." She walked past him to the chair.

"Shall we?" she said, motioning for them to sit. However, no one except for Xavier and Melena sat down.

Tango and Saxton stood by the door with their arms crossed in front of their chests. Edric watched his brothers who stood in similar defensive stances.

"So what's going on?" Xavier asked.

"It's come to my attention, through other means of investigation that Togar Filletto, Count Lumanesque Divanni, and Coriano Morago are planning some sort of infiltration of the circle or at minimum, attempting to steal something of importance to the circle."

"What do you mean? What evidence do you have?" Edric asked.

"Xavier, Saxton, and Tango say that you and your brothers can be trusted, so I am taking their advice and sharing some of my research and findings."

Edric thought she sounded unsure about them. He wished she had more were blood in her so that she would know for certain that he and his brothers were trustworthy and that they could secure her safety and well-being. Instead Gideon gave her one of his annoyed expressions. She stared right back at him and Edric hid his chuckle.

"I was investigating Donovan Kylton as a potential member of the new organization I have been working on to provide impenetrable security for the circle and its members. During my investigation, it came to my attention that he or someone associated with his business, Wolf Bay Banks, is providing some sort of assistance to Filletto, Morago, and Divanni and whatever it is they are working on. I tell you this because I would like you, Xavier, to have your nephews or whomever, monitor these three men. They are up to no good."

"How did you obtain such evidence?" Gideon asked.

Melena turned toward Saxton and Tango. Both men nodded their heads.

"Does it really matter?"

"Yes, it does," Gideon replied.

She looked at Saxton.

"Go ahead, Melena, tell them," Saxton said.

"There was this warehouse, probably the one you and your brothers were investigating, where some paperwork was left lying around. The Wolf Bay Banks symbol was found on a document as well as some other information. That's how we found a connection to Filletto, Divanni, and Morago to Kylton."

Gideon looked at Saxton and Tango.

"Julius warned me about a potential secret society forming. When we got to the warehouse it was empty. What did you find when you and Tango were there?" he asked.

Saxton began to speak but then Melena interrupted.

"It was I who was there. I saw numerous antiques and boxes, some drugs that these men were obviously smuggling inside of the artifacts and documents that talked about an organization. There were sketches of a large building and compound and points of entry."

"You were there? With who? How?" Chance asked as he raised his voice. Edric felt his own temper flare. He didn't like the direction his thoughts were going in. Had Melena snuck into the warehouse alone?

"Listen, that is of no concern of yours. Now, are you going to monitor these individuals or what? Because if you don't, then I won't be able to focus on the job I have to do."

"First of all, sweetheart, we don't take orders from anyone. I want to know why you were there. What were you doing at that warehouse and all alone? Who the hell are you and what are you hiding from us?" Gideon asked, raising his voice.

Melena stood up and closed the file. She pulled another one out of the case and pushed it toward Xavier.

"Can you handle this so that I can take care of my responsibilities?"

Xavier stood up and took the envelope. He stared at Melena.

"You need to be honest with my nephews and I. What is your involvement with this? Why would you go to a warehouse and investigate on your own?"

"I am not at liberty to discuss my job responsibilities to any of you. I'm a big girl, Gideon, and I can take care of myself."

She started to walk away when Gideon grabbed her upper arm to gently stop her. She gasped and looked up toward his face. Edric felt all his brothers' emotions. They were concerned, they were suspicious, and they were getting tired of holding back their emotions about finding their mate. The sooner Melena accepted them, the better.

"Uncle, can you please take Saxton and Tango out of the room and give us a few minutes alone with Melena? There are things we need to discuss."

Melena looked toward Saxton and Tango.

"I'll be fine."

They appeared unsure but nodded toward Melena and exited the room.

* * * *

Melena wasn't sure what Gideon and his brothers were going to do. Right now she should be annoyed, but if she was at all honest with herself, she would admit that she was completely attracted to Gideon and his brothers and aroused by the aggressive way he held her arm.

He stepped closer, lifted her up, and placed her onto the boardroom table. She gasped as her ass hit the hard surface but then leaned back onto the palms of her hands. Gideon placed both of his hands on either side of the table as he leaned over her body. He held her gaze. His deep blue eyes sparkled and seemed to glow a bit.

"We're losing our patience with you. We need to move past the disguises, the limited information and get down to the reality of this relationship."

"What relationship?" she asked and felt the others move around her and the table. One glance around her and she saw the intensity on the men's faces. They were so masculine and sexy and she felt about to freak out and panic.

She felt Gideon's hand move to her waist.

"We can understand your reservations about the five of us. But you need to understand that your existence has immediately opened up an opportunity we thought was lost over a decade ago. We can't take the chance of losing someone so important again."

"We won't take that chance, Melena," Mano added.

She swallowed hard. She wondered what they meant. Had they once loved someone and lost them to death or violence? She felt a mix of emotions as her heart ached and her belly tightened. She was jealous and then she was sad.

"I know what it's like to lose someone close to you. You're right, I don't understand this whole mating thing, but there are more important issues at stake right now. Men like Filletto, Divanni, and Morago must be stopped and destroyed."

She felt Gideon's hand smooth up her waist then her arm and to her shoulder and neck. He cupped her face between his hands and she grabbed onto his forearms.

"You sound like you know them well."

"I know evil and these men represent it in many ways."

"You're going to have to come clean with us, Melena. These men are our enemies. Why are they yours, too?"

She turned away from him and looked toward the blank wall. In her mind, she fought over whether to be completely up front with him or to tell him lies. Even that thought brought on feelings of guilt.

She tried to push off the table but he wouldn't allow it. His much larger body encased hers and she felt his big, hard hands against each thigh on either side of her legs. Melena was completely in tune to his scent, his masculine, superior presence.

"Melena, talk to me. Tell me the truth. Tell me why you seek Morago and these men out."

She closed her eyes and released an uneasy breath. The way Gideon said Morago's name and how compelled she felt to give in to the need to confess to Gideon became too much. Gideon must have felt the same way, because his face moved closer to her. He inhaled against her cheek and her body reacted in a way that shocked her.

He must have smelled her arousal, because the next thing she felt were his hands moving up her body and one cupped her head and hair, making her tilt her chin up toward his face.

Before Melena could pull back, Gideon covered her mouth with his own. He kissed her thoroughly, making love to her mouth, exploring deeply. The feel of his powerful kiss, his take-charge tactics, seemed to ignite something deeper within her. There was no use in fighting it and there was no way she could deny the enticing sensation his kiss caused.

There was no other response for her to give but to kiss him back and enjoy her first kiss with him. When one hand gripped her hair to keep her in place while his other hand moved across her lower back to her waist and pulled her between his splayed thighs, she allowed it and fell into the comfort of Gideon's invasion.

His hard, solid chest pressed against hers and through no recollection of her own, she opened her thighs and he pressed between them. She moaned into his mouth and felt so feverish and wild with need. Thighs of steel pressed into her inner groin. Her heart hammered in her chest, her hands explored his chest and his massive muscular flesh as he deepened the kiss.

Oh my God. Oh my God, I feel my pussy swell and something just leaked from there. Oh God, this is crazy.

The realization of what was happening here brought her out of the fog as embarrassment filled her. She didn't want to come across as easy. This was a crazy, out-of-control situation that had to stop or she would be spread across the table for him to have his way with. That thought aroused her and shocked her as she pulled from his mouth.

"Gideon, stop. Oh God, please, this is too much," she stated as he nuzzled his mouth and face against her neck. His arms wrapped around her and he lifted her up and against him. Gideon continued to lick and suck her skin, sending goose bumps along her flesh. She felt fingertips against her chin then turned toward Mano. He cupped her face between his hands and kissed her hard on the mouth while Gideon continued to kiss along her neck and shoulder bone. It was all too much to handle. Two men kissing her at once while three others looked on waiting for their turn. Her pussy erupted from the thoughts and low growls filtered through the room.

"Listen to your body. Let us show you the ways of the wolf." *Chordeo.*

Mano eased his mouth from hers and before she could open her eyes fully, from being caught in their spell, Chordeo took a turn at kissing her. His thick, large hands cupped her head beneath her hair as he stroked her tongue and kissed her with vigor. She could hardly catch her breath and as he released her lips for Chance to taste her next, she felt Gideon's hand cup her breast and stroke her nipple. "Oh God!" she moaned as she pulled from Chance's mouth.

Edric took his place and pulled her from Gideon's hold. She straddled Edric's waist and he turned her toward the table and laid her back down upon it. In this position as Edric made love to her mouth, he ran his large hand up her skirt, over her thigh to her waist. When he squeezed her hipbone she thrust upward, wanting, needing more. When he finally released her lips and she opened her eyes, she saw Edric's eyes glowing and her heart raced as she gasped. His forearms lay on either side of her head and he smiled down at her.

"See what you've been missing? You belong to us, Melena, and together we're going to prove to you that this is meant to be."

That's what you think. Wait until you find out that revenge is what I'm after. Then you'll want nothing to do with me.

* * * *

They were relentless. Leaning over Melena's shoulder as she looked up information and explained her findings. She was still unsure until Saxton and Tango informed her that the Dolberg brothers were members of the Secret Order of the Brothers of Were. She had been intrigued with the Secret Order for years, since her father was somehow a liaison or informant to members. The group dealings had something to do with his murder, too. Were these wolves capable of showing loyalty to anyone really? For all she knew, Morago had connections on the inside. Why else would he, Divanni, and Filletto still be alive? Especially with their history of criminal activity. Who made the rules? Who decided who lived and who died? What if the Dolberg brothers were involved somehow as members of the Secret Order? After all, weren't their jobs to ensure the safety of the circle and enforce were laws?

She shivered at the thought then felt the hand cover her knee. She jerked a moment until she turned to the right and locked gazes with Edric.

"Are you okay?"

"Yes," she replied then looked back at the screen. Like it wasn't bad enough she couldn't concentrate with these men around her and dressed like a SWAT team about to take on a mission. Hard abs underneath black tight T-shirts and muscular thighs hidden beneath multi-pocketed pants. She knew what those hard thighs felt like, especially against her own thighs like when Gideon spread hers by the conference table.

She gulped hard. These types of thoughts weren't good ones if she wanted to remain focused on the task at hand. Glancing at Edric and his large, thick fingers spread on the table beside her as he looked at her made Melena wonder if he and his brothers were really the good guys. After living with the knowledge she had and only Saxton and Tango to trust, she suddenly felt like she couldn't decide on her own who was trustworthy.

Following her gut had gotten her through different situations. But mix in this seemingly magical sexual desire for these men and she was never so confused in her life.

She hadn't realized that she was still staring at Edric until he spoke to her.

"Melena, I get the feeling that you want to ask me a question. Please, ask me whatever you want. Chance and I will try to ease your mind of the worry."

She looked from Edric to Chance. She knew that Saxton, Tango, Gideon, and Chordeo were trying to decode the letters TAMW as they looked over the drawings of the building and compound she found at the warehouse.

She looked at the screen and a picture she had scanned into the program days ago. The count was onto something important and the fact that she found bills from diggers and exploration teams made her believe that he was searching for artifacts. But what specifically? What artifact could be so important to were packs? She glanced away from the screen and toward Edric. His blue eyes held her gaze and his firm, hard expression made her feel intimidated. She thought about asking him without caring about revealing her knowledge of their position, but she couldn't.

"What is that file?" Chance asked her and Edric moved to her other side. Now both monstrosities of men were hovering.

"It's a series of bills Morago has paid to digging companies. It's like he's searching for something," she replied.

"Maybe artifacts. There were a bunch of things at the warehouse we raided," Edric said. She swallowed hard. If they found out that she was the woman in black who escaped that night, they would surely be pissed off. Look what they did when they discovered she had gone to the other warehouse alone. At least they didn't question her reasoning for taking the set of knives.

"Where are the digs taking place?" Tango asked from the other side of the room.

"Hawaii," Edric said as he took possession of the mouse and keyboard then scanned down the screen. His forearm brushed up against her breast and she jerked backward. It felt like a spark of fire hit her. That move caused her to brush closer against Chance's arm. His large body pressed against her shoulder. Glancing up, she locked gazes with Chance and he winked.

"Melena, it could be he's looking for the book," Saxton said.

She turned toward him.

"You think?"

"What book?" Xavier asked.

"Through intel, we have reason to believe that Morago, Filletto, and Count Divanni are searching for the Book of the Founding Fathers," Saxton stated.

"What?" Gideon asked. His brothers reacted the same way. They were carrying on about what could happen if they found the book and possessed it. They discussed calling Samantha, Ava, and even Dani, their cousins' mate.

"Maybe this has something to do with the person in black that escaped Dashkin and Lunvolk's warehouse while we raided it?" Edric asked.

Oh shit.

Melena felt the need to bolt, but she had to remain calm. She looked at Saxton.

"Hey, I found something on Mercer Collette. He works for Donovan Kylton," Mano called out and she quickly turned toward him. Edric squeezed her knee gently before he stood up and walked toward his brother. They started talking about Mercer and where he could be found.

Melena needed a break. Suddenly her body and her mind were overwhelmed with thoughts of Gideon, Mano, Chordeo, Chance, and Edric. She needed some fresh air and alone time to think. Figuring that Gideon and the others would start looking into Mercer, she decided to flee the room and hit the lady's room.

"Melena, is everything okay?" Saxton asked.

All eyes were upon her.

"Yes. I just need to use the lady's room." He nodded his head and she exited the room.

She entered the bathroom and stared at herself in the mirror. Her cheeks looked flush, her nipples hard. This was not normal. This couldn't be considered normal. She read a lot about were lifestyles and of course Saxton and Tango taught her a lot as well. Could there be such a strong connection and bond between mates that being separated from them caused distress or even pain? Were there really gods that controlled the future and actually decided who engaged in sexual activities or married, well mated actually? She ran her hands through her hair. This was so damn confusing.

She inhaled then exhaled before she exited the bathroom. Walking down the hallway, she decided to peek out the window. It was a gorgeous day and as she looked out toward the side of the building and the park, she saw the large group of people.

She remembered that Filletto and Divanni were going to be part of the ribbon cutting ceremony. They made themselves appear as good citizens of the community but they really weren't. These men needed to be stopped. The killings, the drugs, and the destruction of were law could not happen.

She was going to do something about this. It was odd, but her desire and need to protect the were law and the circle members felt almost as strong as her sexual attraction to Dolberg Pack.

Yikes!

She turned around, ready to head toward the office when she nearly knocked into two men, standing there. They smiled at her and instantly, she knew they were up to no good.

"Oh, excuse me, I didn't see you there. Can I help you?" She looked over their shoulders at the closed office doors. She wondered how they got up here.

"We're looking for you, Melena."

Before she could respond, one of them struck her in the neck with something. She gasped as she covered the spot on her neck with her hand where the syringe had entered. "No!" she yelled or at least she thought she did as her vision began to blur. She fought to remain conscious. This couldn't be happening.

"Let's get her out of here. Take the stairs there."

The door opened, she was still conscious as the one guy carried her down the stairs. Whatever they gave her wasn't to make her pass out. Either that or she had some resistance to the drug.

She screamed aloud, her voice echoed in the stairwell.

* * * *

Julius awoke with a start. He glanced at the clock. It was daytime. It wasn't a dream. Melena was in trouble. He closed his eyes and concentrated. He felt her heartbeat, the flow of her blood, the fear inside of her as she tried to remain alert.

Do you hear me, Melena? Where are you?

At first he got no response. He shouldn't have expected one. He only drank from her blood and of her juices once. But despite his decision to stay clear of her, she was still his intended mate.

Julius?

Yes, Melena. Tell me where you are so I can send help.

Stairwell at work. Two men.

He focused on an image of Gideon then attempted to contact him. Then he pulled the emergency phone from the wall and called Cullen.

"Let me know the moment she is in safekeeping."

"Yes, sir. I will," Cullen said and Julius waited for Melena to give an update. This was torture for him. He could never protect her like she needed protection. She was better off with Gideon and his brothers.

* * * *

Gideon stopped mid-sentence and held his head.

"Melena. She's in trouble." He hurried toward the door. His brothers were with him.

"I smell rogue wolves. They're not from a pack," Edric stated.

"They have our mate. I smell their scent mixed with hers. The staircase," Chance said, and they hurried down the stairwell.

Just as they made it to the last stairwell, they heard the exit door close hard.

Gideon shoved it open, his brothers and Saxton and Tango along with him entered the back parking lot. They caught sight of the two men placing Melena into the white SUV.

Gideon roared in anger that someone tried to take his mate from him. He was about to shift when Saxton stopped him.

"Too many humans around," Saxton warned him.

"Chance is getting the SUV," Mano yelled and just then Chance arrived as the other guys took off in the white SUV.

"We must hurry!" Saxton yelled as they climbed up into the vehicle. As they sped from the parking lot, Gideon called out, "There, five cars ahead. They just took a quick right turn."

"I got it, brother. Ain't no way someone's going to take our mate from us. Never again," Chance said as he skidded around the corner.

Gideon looked at his brothers as they checked their guns. "Got anything for us?" Saxton asked and Chordeo winked as he reached into the back and pulled out a black case. Opening it, he passed two Glocks to Saxton.

"Try these," Chordeo said, but Gideon was having difficulty smiling at his brother's move. His concern was for Melena.

* * * *

Melena attempted to forearm the guy who was on top of her in the backseat of the SUV. Her vision was so blurred that she missed his head and hit his shoulder. He found that amusing. Her frustration at being this affected by the needle they stuck her with pissed her off.

Think, Melena. Think. How do I fight him?

Hit the one in the middle.

She heard the voice in her head and knew it wasn't her own. Or perhaps it was her own and she was just totally losing focus.

Hit the one in the middle. Fight, Melena.

She heard the voice again as the SUV made a sharp right turn nearly making her fall to the floor below the seats. If she did, then he could easily restrain her.

She closed her eyes then felt the man ease up on his hold of her.

God, she wished Gideon or one of the others had gotten to her sooner. She cursed that thought. She was alone as usual. *Just get used to it, Melena. Your destiny lies in loneliness.*

She shoved upward with her hand, pushing the man's face and chin to the right. He hadn't expected that as he moved slightly off of her and she made her move. Throwing her forearm toward the face in the middle of her blurred vision, she felt the hit then pain, but she hit her mark. He moved backward and she jumped up onto her knees and began to pound away at him. At the same time the car swerved, horns honked, and the SUV hit the sidewalk.

She screamed and tried to grab onto the driver seat from the backseat as the second guy drove then lost control and hit the building.

The man who tried to restrain her went to grab her as the first guy jumped out of the SUV. She swung at him numerous times until the door opened wide, the crunching sound of the hinges breaking, indicating that someone with brute force, or in this case wolf strength, pulled it open. A moment later she was alone in the backseat until the men arrived.

* * * *

One of the men shifted. So did Chance and the fight began. As the other man tried to run, Saxton and Tango stopped him.

"Who do you work for?" Saxton asked as he shook the guy.

"No one."

"She's our mate. Why were you trying to take her?" Edric asked as he grabbed the guy from Saxton's hand and shook the man.

"I've got nothing to say."

"Edric, we'll take him and handle this. Can you guys take care of Melena?" Tango asked.

"Of course we can," Edric replied.

"Good. We'll let you know what we find out," Saxton said. He and Tango took the guys to the side of the building. Another vehicle approached. Xavier was driving.

"Is she okay, Gideon?" Edric asked as he joined his brothers by Melena. She was lying down in the SUV.

"I'm fine. My head is fuzzy and I can't see straight," she replied.

"Did they hit you?" Chance asked and she shook her head.

"They stuck me with a needle."

They mumbled curses as Gideon pulled her into his arms. "Have the men run this vehicle and find out the owner." He carried Melena toward another vehicle by the side of the building.

"Hey, how the hell did you know that she was in trouble?" Mano asked Gideon.

"I didn't. Not until Julius whispered it in my head," he said, shocking his brothers. He heard Melena gasp but then she turned away and looked out the window.

Chapter 12

"What do you mean Wilton wasn't successful?" Divanni asked as he looked around the park, waiting for the SUV to show up with the beautiful Melena inside.

"They were taken into custody by two men and Dolberg Pack," Colin stated into the cell phone.

"Dolberg Pack? Why do they keep showing up around Melena?"

"It seems that she is of importance to them. The two men must have called in Fagan Pack for backup. Their mate Dani, along with three of the five brothers are inside the building."

"Fuck. I hope Wilton keeps his mouth shut. This could destroy the plan completely. I need to find out who Melena is as well as the two wolves. Send me pictures so I can pass them along to Morago."

"Yes, sir."

Divanni hung up the phone and waited for his driver. This was not good at all. "Who is Melena and why is she so important to Dolberg and Xavier?"

* * * *

Melena knew that the men surrounded her and that she was lying on a bed. It was better to keep her eyes closed than to face them right now with her vision still blurred and her body weak from whatever those men stuck her with.

She felt the bed dip. Not just on one side but all around her. Opening her eyes, she could see them all there, but their images were blurry.

She kept blinking.

"We think they gave you some sort of sedative, but you were somehow able to resist it. It should wear off soon," Chordeo whispered and she thought he looked angry. Maybe it was just the blurriness.

"Don't be angry. Everything worked out," she whispered, and he released an annoyed sigh.

She should really try to stand up, but as she attempted to rise, she felt the large, warm palm over her belly and fell back down onto the pillow.

"Lie down and relax. We'll take care of you." *Gideon. God, you're so demanding and bossy.*

"I should try to sit up and clear my head."

"No, just lie down and let us take care of you." Mano spoke this time, and then she felt the hand caress against her ankle and calf. She realized that her high heels were gone and her breathing suddenly felt shaky.

"I'm okay. Really, I am," she stuttered then attempted to run fingers through her hair in a nervous manner but missed her hairline and instead poked herself in the eye.

"Ouch."

"Hey, just relax. It may take some time for your vision to clear and the drugs to wear off." Gideon took her fingers and brought them to his lips. He kissed each one as Chance leaned on the bed on the other side of her and drew circles on the palm of her other hand.

She could hardly breathe from the excitement that exploded through her body.

"I'm okay."

"You keep saying that. But we want to make sure," Chance stated and she felt Mano's hands move further up her legs then back down again.

Gideon leaned down and whispered next to her ear. "You scared me, sweet Melena. I thought I lost you."

He continued to spread tiny kisses along her ear and jaw then over her lips. His kisses were soft, yet seemed to increase with every stroke. She found herself turning toward him and ultimately landing against his chest. His hands caressed over her lower back and the reality of his large size began to sink in. The man, the men were monstrous in comparison to her. Yet, here she was, fully absorbing Gideon's embrace and caress.

He explored her mouth while his hands explored her body. The moment his palm moved under the fabric of her blouse she pulled from his mouth.

He gripped her tighter, nearly taking the breath from her. She pressed her palms against his chest and held his gaze. His blue eyes glowed, showing his wolf.

"Please don't hurt me," she whispered.

"Never," he replied, and she closed her eyes and tried to calm her breathing. How did the situation grow so out of control so quickly? Hadn't she questioned their loyalty to were law, to authority, to her, only a short time ago? Everything she had learned thus far about wolves, about the Secret Order indicated a breakdown in command, in abiding by laws and protecting their own. How would she know if they were part of the problem and the lapse in security years ago that killed her family or if they could be trusted now?

He leaned down and kissed her again, momentarily making her forget what she had been thinking or why she was even fighting this attraction.

He moved his hand along her waist, past her ribs and right to her breast. When he cupped the mound, she moaned into his mouth and he deepened the kiss. She ached now in both breasts and pushed upward against his hand. When Gideon brushed his thumb back and forth across her nipple then pulled the tip between finger and thumb, she moaned louder, her body tightening up.

Gideon pulled from her mouth and held her gaze with a cocky, experienced expression.

"I need you, Melena. We all do."

The reality of his words reminded her of the audience around them. She looked at them and each of their serious expressions and she felt the tears reach her eyes. Every part of her body told her that this was right, but her mind, her broken heart, the fear of trusting anyone other than Saxton and Tango had her grabbing Gideon's hand. Taking into account the fact that she had never been this close, this intimate with any man before and now five sat before her in a bedroom, and yes, she was freaking out.

She felt her breathing grow rapid. She nearly jerked her ankle free as Mano continued to caress her skin. She felt them everywhere on every bit of her skin and body. *How the hell could this be happening to me?*

Gideon looked at her with deep, dark eyes of sexuality. She didn't need to know about sex to know that this man wanted her and so did his brothers. She was panicking big-time as she thought about their size, their bodies, and their cocks.

"Please, Gideon. I don't think I'm ready for this. I hardly know any of you. I feel so confused," she admitted and he leaned on his side and began to slowly undo the buttons on her blouse. Chance touched a finger to her jaw so she would look up at him.

"Don't be scared of us. As your mates, we would never hurt you. We'll go slow, Melena."

"As slow as you need us to," Gideon added as her blouse parted revealing her silk off-white bra. The men inhaled.

"By the gods, you are beautiful, woman," Chordeo said from the left side of the bed.

She nibbled her bottom lip and Gideon brushed his thumb across her breast. "Let us show you how good it will be." He reached down and began to push his hand up between her thighs. She held his gaze, her lips parted, and she felt her legs begin to shake.

She wanted this. She had been in sexual arousal since seeing them in their SWAT team attire in the conference room.

Her sexual needs also stemmed from Julius's touch. Her heart ached. She felt as if she were betraying him, but Julius wasn't her mate. These men were her intended mates. They were her destiny. Julius obviously wasn't or he would be here right now.

"Open for him, Melena," Edric said as he joined them by her left thigh. Now all five men surrounded her on the bed and then she felt Gideon's fingers over her panties and against her mound. She reached down to grab his wrist and stop him from removing her panties.

"Please, Gideon."

"It will be okay," Chordeo said as he glided his hands up her thighs and reached her panties. Gideon moved his hand a moment and Chordeo pulled her panties from her body. She felt the gush of cream leak from her pussy and all five men growled low. Gideon immediately placed two fingers to her pussy and pushed upward.

"Oh, Gideon, what are you doing?" She grabbed for whatever was in reach. Chance held her wrist and brought it above her head, then kissed her deeply. She grabbed onto Gideon's shoulder as he continued to thrust his fingers in and out of her pussy while Chance devoured her moans. She felt Gideon's thick, wide thumb press against her sensitive flesh and she moaned into Chance's mouth. Her hips thrust upward and then she felt Gideon shift his body between her legs. Mano was there to take Gideon's place as he placed her other arm above her head so her breasts pushed forward. He and Chance each cupped a breast with their free hand as Chance released her lips.

Gideon stroked her pussy and played with her clit as Mano moved lower for a kiss. She was completely turned on and knew she was going to come.

She gasped for air as Chance and Mano unclipped her bra, releasing her needy breasts from confinement.

"You're gorgeous, woman," Chance stated.

"And all ours to feast on," Mano added before leaning down and taking a nipple between his lips. She felt the imaginary string from nipples to her pussy.

"Oh!" she moaned louder. Their touch was too much, too powerful to fight, but why would she. It was incredible.

Gideon ran the palm of his hand up over her belly then back down as he continued to thrust his fingers into her.

"So responsive and wet. I need to taste you."

"I need to taste her, too," Edric added then smiled. Her vision was improving as Gideon lowered to his chest, lifted her thighs and replaced his fingers with his tongue.

"Oh, Gideon!"

She felt overwhelmed with emotions as Chance and Mano leaned down and began to feast on her breasts with tongues, teeth, and mouth in sync to Gideon's ministrations.

Her heart raced as she absorbed the men, her men and their individuality. She wanted to run her fingers through Chance's crew-cut hair. She imagined riding Mano as she gripped his shoulder length hair and took control of his sexy body. Her mouth opened, her eyes closed and she thrust forward in response to her thoughts.

Gideon had his own interpretation of her moans and actions.

"Gideon." She said his name as he lifted her rear.

Her legs were over Gideon's large, wide shoulders. She felt his tongue move back and forth over the slit of her pussy then to her anus. She gasped and lifted up, while pressing her heels into his muscular shoulders. He didn't seem to mind one bit as Gideon continued to feast on her.

Chin to chest she photographed his image in her mind. The intensity of his face, the veins against his temples as he ate at her cream and the way his muscles felt hard and demanding beneath the back of her thighs.

"That's it, baby. You look like a goddess," Chance complimented.

Every lick and suck with their mouths and tongues brought her body to another level. They moaned as they indulged in her body making her feel so sexy and provocative. Never in her imagination would she think that foreplay would be like this. And she knew this was what they were doing. They were preparing her body for sex and suddenly she didn't feel so scared as she felt needy for more of them.

She placed her hands onto Chance's and Mano's heads. She widened her thighs. The need for more was overwhelming.

"Yes, oh God, yes, please."

Gideon's tongue took that special little route, sliding between her pussy lips, straight to her puckered hole and she shivered as she combusted.

Melena felt her entire body tighten, and then she exploded in pleasure as she turned her head side to side and shook in the aftereffects. Gideon rose up, kissing her inner thighs and smiling before he moved out of the way and Chordeo took his place. Her chest rose and fell.

"It's torture smelling your sweet cream and waiting to sample it."

She felt her cheeks warm as embarrassment overtook her and the men chuckled. Chance cupped her chin and kissed her lips.

"No need to be shy, baby. This body, these breasts, this pussy is ours."

"Oh. My. God," she replied as Chordeo latched onto her pussy lips and nipped her clit. She jerked her hips and the man began to stroke her pussy and alternate fingers then tongue. The slight dusting of whiskers on his cheeks tickled her skin and aroused her senses. She wiggled and pleaded for mercy. It was too much. She closed her eyes and absorbed the sensation thinking that this was way better than just reading about sex.

As the thought hit her, she realized that sex would be next with them. Sex with five huge Alpha males.

Chance and Mano moved out of the way and Gideon and Edric took their place. They both latched onto her breasts and stroked her thighs, opening them wider to Chordeo. Even the feel of their large, splayed palms and fingers against her quivering thighs aroused some inner feminine characteristic inside of her. She felt empowered, lustful, and wanton.

She inhaled her own scent and the mix of masculinity around her. Something brewed stronger inside of her. She wasn't afraid to lose her virginity to these men, but she was afraid to open up her heart for pain. But as Chordeo and the men aroused her senses and brought her to new heights, her fear of pain diminished and instead bolts of bright light and some sort of inner explosion occurred and she screamed out in bliss while Gideon, Chance, Mano, Chordeo, and Edric talked her through it and ultimately began to open up her heart.

* * * *

Gideon never felt so possessive or hungry in his entire life. To know that he and his brothers were given this second chance in life with a new mate was so unheard of and such a gift he was in awe of Melena. She was someone very special. Not just because she was their woman and mate, but because of her position in securing the circle and were law and creating the Security Ring. As members of the Secret Order, they swore to protect the laws for eternity and now their mate was helping to do just that.

"I agree with you, Gideon. She is more special than words can describe," Edric added and his brothers added similar comments through their shared mind link. It was amazing to have such a connection and ability and even now, as they prepared Melena to be made love to by them, he already felt a bond begin to form.

"Delicious," Chordeo stated then lifted up and began to pull her skirt from her body. Melena reached down, pulling from Chance and Mano's hands and covered her mound.

"No more. That was too much. Please."

Gideon stood up. "You're our woman, Melena. We need to seal the bond between the six of us. It will help to protect you and it will calm our wolves." He pulled off his shirt and began to undo the zipper to his pants.

"Oh God, you mean sex. You want to have sex right now? I hardly know you. Any of you," she replied in a panicky voice. God, she was so adorable and youthful. She was young and inexperienced, and this was what caused her fear.

"We will take things slowly, Melena. This is how we seal the bond between us. The gods have chosen you for us and us for you," Chordeo said then smoothed his hands up her thighs, parting them. She remained covering her pussy with her hands and Gideon chuckled. He pushed his pants down and his brothers began to undress, too. She closed her eyes.

"Oh God, I'm not ready. I don't know what to do."

As Gideon placed his hand over her belly she jerked to the side and her eyes popped open. He watched her eyes, as they zeroed in on his chest then lower until her beautiful green eyes widened like saucers. His cock grew harder and longer.

"This is yours. I belong to you as you belong to my brothers and me." He fisted his cock in his hands then stepped between her thighs and parted them.

"I think I should tell you that I don't know what to do and that I'm rather freaked out right now."

"It's okay. I know I'm big, but I'll fit. You're meant for me."

She swallowed hard and Gideon eased over her.

"Let me make love to you, Melena. Today we all will seal our bond."

"I'm a virgin," she blurted out and then he smiled.

"I figured as much. You saved yourself for us. There will never be anyone else, ever." He leaned down and kissed her lips and stroked his cock back and forth against her fingers. She touched his cock, and he had to pull from his inner willpower not to explode against her delicate fingers. The trembling of her hand, her delicate touch was nearly too much for him. She was special.

"Sweet lover, you're killing me. Let me in. Let me take your virginity and make you ours."

She opened her thighs wider, wrapped her arms around his shoulders and held his gaze. He could see the tears in her eyes and he wondered if it were sadness. But then she smiled as her lower lip quivered. He felt her fingertips gently run through his hair and against his scalp. In this moment, he knew she would belong to him forever and would hold his heart in her hands.

"I don't know if my gut is right or wrong, but I hope it's right, Gideon. Make love to me. I want you to."

He took that moment to ease into her, slowly pushing through that sacred barrier. If there was any doubt in his mind that she was telling the truth, he knew better now. She had never opened her thighs to any other man and she would only make love to him and his brothers. Such a deep feeling of possessiveness and need roared through his body. He felt his cock harden and grow within her. Melena gasped for breath, moaning and trying to widen her thighs for him. As her fingers pressed against his ass, he lost all control to move slow and shoved into her, taking Melena's breath away. She didn't scream in pain or try to get free. Instead she leaned closer to his neck and kissed then nibbled on his skin. It drove him wild with desire as he made love to her with his brothers, his pack mates all around them.

With every stroke she grew wetter and moaned for more. He increased his thrusts until he couldn't hold back. He felt her pussy muscles tighten and grip his cock, and then she screamed her release and he followed as he came inside of her.

He held her in his arms and kissed her shoulders, her neck and cheek until he reached her lips.

"Are you okay?" he asked her and she nodded her head.

"Very okay, Gideon."

* * * *

Gideon gave her a few minutes to calm her breathing and accept his brothers next. He caressed her silky thighs, gave her hip bone a squeeze before he moved from between her legs, and allowed his brothers to claim her as well. Chance moved in behind her and began to massage her shoulders then her ass.

"Chance needs you, Melena, so do all my brothers."

She smiled at him and Chance hugged her close.

"I can't wait, baby. Can't wait." Gideon got up and Chance rolled her to her back and straddled her waist.

"Mine now," he whispered, and she smiled then reached up and cupped his cheek in her hand.

"You're so handsome," she whispered and he smiled.

Chance played with her nipples, pulling and teasing her until she thrust her hips upward.

"That's it, baby. You like that?"

"Yes," she replied as he stroked his thumb and forefinger over her nipples, pulling, plucking, and massaging them. She held his gaze, staring deeply into his eyes, and he could see how turned on she was getting.

He saw her eyes widen as she stared at his cock that lay over her belly.

"You can touch my cock, baby. It's all yours to explore." He saw her cheeks redden. She was so innocent and sweet. How the hell did the gods decide to grant them such a treasure? They were wild and untamed in so many ways. The fact that they were moving this slow and enjoying the pleasure told him a lot. She was special and this connection and commitment were forever.

When her fingers touched his cock, Chance closed his eyes and moaned. Her delicate fingers caressed along the tip. The mushroom top felt so incredibly sensitive he tightened his thighs and willed his beast to grab Melena, press her to the bed, and fuck her until he calmed his beast. But then the little innocent minx cupped his balls.

"Oh damn, Melena. That feels incredible. So fucking sexy. I need to be inside of you, baby. You keep touching me and I'm going to explode right here."

He got into position between her thighs. He lifted her up from under her knees and she squealed as he adjusted her thighs over his thighs.

"I want access to this ass when I'm inside this pussy, woman."

"Oh my God, Chance, what do you mean?"

He had to hide the chuckle at her pure question. She hadn't a clue about mating, making love, having sex with a man, never mind a wolf. He wanted to squeeze her to him and possess her forever and shelter her from the pain and realities of life.

"You're mine, woman. That means every part of you."

He pressed a finger down her cunt to her puckered hole and she nearly shot up off the bed. Instead, with her thighs over his thick, solid ones, the move made her seem as though she wanted his finger in her ass.

"Nice and easy. You're mine to take and have forever."

He eased his cock through her tight vaginal muscles as he clenched his teeth. She felt so tight and amazing he thought he might explode before he was fully inside of her.

"Hot damn, woman, you are tight. So fucking tight."

She gripped his forearms and tilted her breasts upward.

"You're too big. Oh God, I don't know if I can."

He smiled at her and nibbled his bottom lip as he stared at her breasts. He immediately felt her pussy leak and he smiled.

"I'm going to taste every fucking part of you."

"Oh!" She moaned then closed her eyes and tilted her head back.

He reached down and ran a finger over her pussy lips, gathering some cream before he reached her puckered hole.

Melena gasped and tightened up as a flow of cream lubricated his cock sending him completely balls deep inside of her.

"Fuck yeah."

He stroked his finger back and forth over her puckered hole as he thrust his cock into her pussy.

He knew he wouldn't last. That angelic face, lips parted, little moans escaping from her lips and her fingernails dug into his thighs. Her large breasts bounced with every thrust of his cock into her pussy. It was all too much.

He increased his thrusts and exploded inside of her, calling her name before he shook from the intensity.

"Beautiful." He leaned down and kissed her as he pulled slowly from her body.

* * * *

Melena closed her eyes and tried to register such sexually charged men. She wasn't certain she could handle them, but as Chance eased out of her, Chordeo was there pulling her into his arms and cuddling her close to his chest. Who would have thought that the first time she had sex, she would also allow anal touch? She was now contemplating, wondering what it would feel like to have a cock in her ass. *Holy shit, I must be losing my mind. Maybe it's overrated. Maybe books lie and enhance that type of thing.*

She swallowed hard as she absorbed the situation for what it was. There was no explaining the deep pull within her. The way her mind tried to evaluate the situation and analyze why she accepted having sex with five men she hardly knew at all, yet felt she knew entirely. Gideon had been so gentle and passionate. It was different than his dominating personality. To think that he had intimidated her at first but now intrigued her was mind altering itself.

Now Chance, Chance she totally understood. He was slick, charming, flirtatious, and bulky. His short crew-cut hair was the only immediate difference in appearance to his brother Gideon, whose hair was to his shoulder in waves of onyx.

"You got awfully quiet, Melena. Talk to me," Chordeo whispered, pulling her from her own thoughts. Getting lost in her mind was habitual and comforting whenever she felt out of sorts.

She glided her palm up his chest and to his face. She couldn't believe that these men were hers. Would they truly be mated for life? Was that even possible to love someone for that long? She licked her lips and he watched them roll over her lower lip. She felt a spark of excitement and power. It was feminine and completely shocking to her. Why did she want to act sexy for him, for them?

He turned his cheek and kissed her palm as someone joined them on the bed. Hard lips gently touched her shoulder before she felt the teeth glide along her collarbone to her neck. She giggled from the tickle and looked up to the side to see Edric's dark blue eyes and firm cheekbones. The man was extra large, in all the right places. She felt his cock tap against her rear as he slid up and down. She tensed up.

Chordeo cupped her breasts then leaned down to lick across her nipple as Edric placed a hand on her hip then slid it between her thighs.

She leaned back against him and allowed them to lead her on this journey. They were so talented. Their lips, their tongues and teeth, and of course their cocks.

Edric raised her thigh back and up over his thigh before he pressed a finger to her pussy.

"Oh, Edric."

"Feel good, baby?"

"Yes."

Chordeo inhaled as he lowered his head and began to lick a trail across each breast, down her abdomen to her pussy. Everywhere his lips brushed across, she felt an imaginary string run through her body, embrace her heart and connect her soul to them. Firm lips, warm, moist kisses soothed fears that were deep and buried within her.

Uncertainty caused her to waver only momentarily until Chordeo's mouth reached her pussy.

"You smell like heaven on earth."

She reached back to touch Edric as Chordeo licked across her folds then plunged his tongue inside of her.

She gripped Edric's hair and he plucked her nipples.

"So wet and sexy. The gods have blessed us with the perfect woman."

She closed her eyes as Chordeo did something amazing with his tongue and fingers to her cunt. She felt out of control, needy beyond satisfaction until he pulled away and Edric lined his cock up to her pussy from behind then shoved forward.

She gasped as she reached forward only for Edric to stop her with firm words.

"Keep those arms up and spread your thighs for me and Chordeo." She did as she was told, which totally turned her on and caused a gush of cream to leak from her pussy.

"That's right, baby. You listen to your Alphas and we'll give you pleasure," Chordeo said as he held his cock in his hand and stroked it.

"She's so tight. I can't hold back," Edric mumbled as he rolled her to her belly, wrapped an arm around her midsection to help raise her to all fours, then began stroking into her from behind.

Melena grabbed the comforter and fisted the fabric between her hands as a wave of emotions and feelings consumed her.

In this position, on all fours, vulnerable to Edric's ministrations she realized was an act of acceptance to their dominance and control. Unlike days, hours earlier, when the idea of being possessed by them felt insulting, degrading almost, but now it was different. They weren't dominating her to make her weak. They were making love to her, possessing her, laying each of their imprints on her so that everyone from here on out knew she was their mate.

She was completely in tune to her body and what these men were doing to her. Her pussy felt needy, her breasts full and sensitive as they bounced with every thrust from Edric.

"Harder, Edric. I need more," she yelled, and he thrust faster, holding her in place, his arm like a vise grip around her midsection and under her breasts. She felt hungry as she counterthrust backward until Edric shoved in deep and exploded inside of her.

"Damn, woman, that was hot. Yes." He cheered her on as he slowly eased out of her and kissed her spine.

She was going to turn around, but Chordeo stopped her.

"Stay right there. It's my turn."

Without warning he positioned himself behind her and shoved inside of her making her gasp at the sudden thrust. Chordeo was quiet and intense. His lack of making a spectacle of himself or leading her to believe he was just like his brothers caught her off guard. He was different. He was the unexpected, and right now, she was ready to challenge him in return. She was ready to leave her mark, her indication to them that they belonged to her as she belonged to them.

In and out he stroked her pussy and played with her breasts. His large, thick thighs slapped against her thighs with every deep stroke.

"Yes, yes, more, Chordeo…more."

When she felt his finger against her puckered hole, she tightened up and he thrust into her.

"Not so mouthy and demanding now, mate, are ya?"

"Oh, Chordeo." She moaned then felt his finger push through the tight rings of her ass. It was exactly what her body needed. She was hungry, needy in a way she couldn't explain or define. Chordeo seemed to understand that which made her accept his possession of her in any way.

"Oh God, that's naughty. It's too much. I never."

He leaned down over her shoulder and whispered into her ear as he sucked on her earlobe.

"You will. One day real soon, you're going to get a cock in your ass, Melena. My cock."

He thrust into her two more times as she shook from his words and his strokes. Chordeo exploded inside of her.

* * * *

Mano lifted Melena up and carried her out of the bedroom and into the shower.

She leaned back against the shower wall and closed her eyes.

"I can't move. I feel so relaxed and exhausted."

Mano chuckled then cupped her breasts with his hands. Their woman was voluptuous and sexy.

"I will take care of you now and then we'll rest." He leaned forward to kiss her and his sweet woman, despite exhaustion, kissed him back. When her arms wrapped around his shoulders, he had to have her.

"I need you, baby. I need you like my brothers."

"I know, Mano. I want to. Help me."

He lifted her up and pressed her against the wall as her legs parted. He could feel them shaking. His brothers had made love to her exquisitely and now the poor, sweet woman was exhausted. He would need to go slowly this first time. She needed passion and some restraint.

He explored her mouth as the water cascaded over them. Her silky, muscular thighs moved against his outer thighs and waist. He squeezed her to him.

The feel of her lips, full and luscious, were a tasty treat, but her cream, the scent of her called to his wolf as much as the man in him.

Reaching down between them, Melena shocked him when she held his cock with her delicate hands and aligned it with her pussy.

He locked gazes with her green eyes.

"You're okay?"

He couldn't believe he was asking her that. In the past, he took what he wanted from a woman and when he wanted it. Melena was different, not because she was his mate, but because of the woman she was and how she handled herself. He was impressed with her, proud to have her as a mate and desperate to mark her and bind them forever.

"Very okay, Mano. Make love to me. I want you. Is that okay?"

He smiled at her then squeezed her to him as his cock hardened from her words.

"Very okay. I'm yours now."

He pressed forward, her words encouraging as they provided him strength and confirmed their mutual desire for one another. He made love to her slowly. They held gazes as she gripped his shoulders and pushed downward as he pushed upward.

"Just like that, Melena. You are a natural at seduction."

She blushed and he thrust a little harder and a little faster.

"So shy and innocent."

"Not anymore," she replied then counterthrust against him.

"Enough talking." He gripped her hips and stroked her pussy in hard fast thrusts. He looked down between their bodies, admired her full breasts as the water dripped from delicious pink nipples. He licked his lips, allowed his cock to push deeper. He loved the sight of his cock disappearing into her pussy, the way his large hands gripped her hip bones. He caught his breath as his heart soared with admiration of his woman.

Over and over again he penetrated deeper, making her moan louder and eventually scream her release. His wolf nearly howled in relief itself as the satisfaction of finding its mate and securing the bond was completed. They had a mate and she was stunning and beautiful, and yes, filled with secrets they would have to coax from her as they gained her full trust.

Chapter 13

"We know who you work for. Just give us some information and we'll let you live," Saxton told Wilton as he, Van, Tango, and Miele tried to get him to snitch on Count Divanni.

"I don't know what you're talking about," Wilton said with a smug expression.

"You're going to jail and you're going before the council to be punished for your crimes," Van said.

"There's a process with that. Send me now," he replied. Saxton thought the guy was overly confident.

"No one is going to bail you out. You're a risk to the count now. I wouldn't be surprised if he had you knocked off before you reached prison," Miele added.

"Go to hell, loser. You're nothing."

"Oh, I'm something and you're going to be prime meat when you hit that cell. There's no shifting. The doctors give you a shot that stops your ability to shift. It's torture to lay there and not be free. No running in the woods, howling at the moon. You're done," Van said.

Wilton looked at Saxton and the others.

"I don't think so. I'll last the week and after that, you'll be dead and I'll be free."

Saxton was pissed. They had been at this for hours.

"Lock him up. We'll see what the council wants to do," Van stated and two other guards escorted the prisoner from the room.

"So, you've been keeping our cousin's mate under lock and key for quite some time. Who is she really?" Van asked as Miele took a seat and then Randolph, Bently, and Baher joined them.

"I don't like this," Saxton stated.

"I don't either. He sounded awfully cocky and like he knew something was coming," Tango added.

"You can't change the subject. Besides, we know something is coming. Dani and Sam have been on the phone back and forth for the last three days. So who is this Melena?" Van asked as Dani entered the room.

"She's the one we've been waiting for. There's going to be some massive trouble headed our way. Melena needs to be protected at all costs," Dani said and all the men stared at her.

"Are our cousins in danger?" Miele asked.

Dani nodded her head.

"It looks like Melena was onto something when she came across that information at the warehouse. Sam has had some unfamiliar faces hanging around Wolf City and I've noticed a few people moving up the department ladder rather fast. These guys are good. They've planted some informants," Dani said.

"What? How the hell could they do that under our noses?" Bently asked.

"Morago is a major threat to the circle. He has made a lot of money in the US and overseas. My latest intel says he is planning some big trip in a week to Hawaii."

"Hawaii?" Saxton asked, immediately not liking where this information was heading.

"Yes, he's up to something with the count and Filletto. Mercer Collette has been acting strangely and we believe he is being used to frame Donovan Kylton for whatever wrongdoing Morago is responsible for," Dani told them.

"Holy shit," Tango said.

"We need to protect Melena and she needs to finish securing the Ring. Morago, Filletto, and Divanni could be trying to locate the Book of the Founding Fathers," Saxton said.

"That is what Sam, Ava, and I were discussing as a possibility. Does Melena still hold the key?"

Saxton nodded his head.

"The key to what? The book?" Van asked and Dani nodded her head.

"I know. She's lost so much already. We all need her to remain safe," Dani said.

Saxton had the feeling that something very bad was about to happen.

* * * *

"Where did you get these pictures?" Morago asked the count.

"I had my men take them. No one recognized these two."

"They disappeared years ago. They were part of a secret organization once," Morago said as he thought about Zeikele Mahalan. Killing him and his family secured their property and the treasure. He never would have been able to save enough money and build the army that he did, if Zeikele had been successful in blowing his illegal activities.

"Are they a concern?" the count asked.

"They could be. Are there more pictures? Where is the one of the woman you seem to be obsessed with?"

The count hesitated, passing them over to Morago.

He squinted his eyes and looked over the pictures. She looked familiar, yet he didn't think he actually knew her or had seen her ever before.

"Who is she?"

"Someone of great importance to Xavier, the Dolberg Pack, and it seems the circle, too. Wilton is being held under high security at the prison."

Morago looked up from the picture to the count. "She is quite beautiful. Do you think Wilton will cave in?"

"No. He'd rather die than deal with the consequences of being a rat."

"Good. I think we need to get the Dolberg Pack, Fagan Pack, and the circle to focus on something else so we can make our move. What would impact them greatly?"

"An attack on Sam or Lord Crespin. Maybe abducting Donovan Kylton."

"I was thinking about getting our hands on this woman. She could be important if that many higher-ups are securing her. Take out Saxton and Tango. They'll only stand in your way of succeeding."

* * * *

Melena was starving and so were the guys. They cooked some burgers, ate, then waited to hear from Tango and Saxton.

Melena stood up and wiped down the counter as the men cleaned up, too. She was leaning against the counter when Mano pulled her into his arms and clasped his hands behind her back. She laid her head on his chest and closed her eyes. It felt amazing to be held by him. She felt safe.

"Where have you been hiding?" he asked her.

She looked up, feeling a bit guilty and surprised by his question even though he was sort of smiling. "What do you mean, Mano?"

He stroked her cheek with the back of his hand. For such big men, they were very gentle when it came to her.

"You appeared out of nowhere. You've worked for our uncle, remaining hidden in the basement office for the past three years. Why? What was with all the secrets and disguises?"

She swallowed hard as she lowered her eyes. She didn't want to lie to them. She didn't want their relationship to start out this way. They could truly help her make a difference and stop Morago, Filletto, and the count from destroying the circle. But her identity as the Goddess of the circle needed to remain secure. At least for now, while the Security Ring was still being established.

"I guess the best answer I can give you is that Saxton and Tango felt I needed protection. I lost many family members when I was young, and Saxton and Tango raised me and taught me how to survive and defend myself. I guess staying hidden under a wig, and in the basement offices, provided extra security to me."

His fingers clutched her chin causing her to look up into his blue eyes.

"You're too beautiful to hide."

She smiled as he kissed her softly on the lips. Gideon's cell phone rang and she stepped from Mano's arms only for Chordeo to grab her and pull her close. He was nuzzling her neck when Gideon spoke.

"That was Saxton. They want to meet up in a secure location. They didn't get anything from Divanni's man. Dani and our cousins are with them. They have some insight into the operation and Divanni. Filletto and Morago are conspiring. They feel he may be going after the Book of the Founding Fathers."

"We need to go," Melena said as she pulled from Chordeo's arms.

"Wait. I'm worried that they may try to take you," Gideon stated.

"I need to go. I need to be with Saxton and Tango." She grabbed her jacket. Chance pulled her toward him and she gasped at the unexpected grab.

"What's going on between you, Saxton, and Tango? You said they raised you."

"They did, Chance. There's nothing sexual between the three of us. They're the only family I have and I would do anything for them."

"Okay." He turned her around so he could help her get her jacket on. She was totally caught off guard at the gesture, and as she smiled to herself at his gentlemanlike behavior, he smacked her on the ass. "Let's move."

* * * *

It was dark out. Melena usually had trouble seeing in the dark, but oddly enough, she felt as if her vision was almost clear. Kind of like night vision. She could make out things she normally couldn't. Gideon and Mano were on either side of her. Chordeo and Chance were somewhere ahead of them and Edric was a good distance behind her. She didn't like the feeling she had or the eeriness to the air. It smelled like rain was coming. That damp, cool air that gave her chills. It seeped through her jacket.

"Are you cold, mate?" Mano asked as he took her hand and brought it to his lips.

The way he called her mate, held her eyes with his glowing wolf ones, gave her a sensation of protection. Then came the fear.

They were right outside of the building. Her building. The safe house for her, Saxton and Tango. She jumped and instinctively grabbed onto Mano as she heard the growl and then what sounded like garbage pails falling over. Turning her head left and right as Mano pulled her against his chest, she could see the glowing eyes and then all hell broke loose.

"Morago's men," Mano whispered and she gasped as fear overtook the secure feelings from moments ago.

* * * *

Saxton and Tango didn't have time to warn the others. In a flash men were infiltrating the building. They exited from the back and immediately saw men shift into wolf form. They could smell Melena's scent and if they could, so could the others.

"Where is she? Do you see her?" Tango asked and Saxton could hear the concern and fear in his friend's voice.

"No, but I smell her scent. It's so strong. Much stronger than normal."

"They began the mating process. Her men will protect her."

"They'll need us, Tango. Knowing Melena, she hasn't told them who she really is."

The growl came out of nowhere as the large black wolf leaped at Tango. Saxton roared as he grabbed the wolf off his friend and shifted. They tumbled to the ground as more roars and fighting filled the air. Where was Melena?

By the gods, keep her safe.

* * * *

"Melena, stay right here and don't move. I can't protect you if you don't listen to me," Mano whispered with teeth clenched.

Fear and anger were beginning to build up into her chest.

"They need me. Saxton and Tango need help."

"Gideon and the others are on it. You stay here with me."

She heard the roars, the cries of pain as flesh was torn from bodies. Shaking her head she covered her ears and cried. *Not again. Please protect Saxton and Tango. Please, whomever is in charge, protect my mates.*

She tumbled over as the large wolf attacked Mano. Falling to the ground she hit the pavement hard, her flesh torn as she cried out.

Melena back crawled away from the fighting wolves. In a panic she looked around her, could somehow see the images of wolves fighting. All her men were fighting and then she saw the two bodies on the ground. *Saxton, Tango…no.*

She had to get to them. *They can't be dead, oh God, please keep them alive. I need them.*

As she stood up another wolf went to grab her, scraping its claw against her arm as she quickly evaded his grasp. She reached around for a weapon, anything to protect herself when the wolf lunged toward her again. Just as she saw its teeth and thought it was going to kill her, the hand reached out from behind her and crushed the beast's throat. The mess of fur and bones fell to the cement with a thump. She turned to see who was there when the cape came around her body, blocking her from seeing anything but darkness. Inhaling as she gasped in fear, she smelled the familiar, masculine scent. Then strong arms wrapped around her.

"You're safe, my love. They cannot harm you now."

Julius?

She tried to pull away, but his hold was binding and he wouldn't allow it. Her cheek was nearly crushed to his chest. Her arms stuck around his midsection where she couldn't move, yet his hands roamed over her body freely. He was using his powers on her again. Why did he keep doing this?

"I need to help them. Saxton and Tango need me."

"He's out there. Morago waits in the shadows. He cannot have you, Melena. If he figures out whom you are, he will try to possess you and stake claim to a throne he doesn't deserve and one he will destroy. Your mates will die. Even I will die if these men succeed."

She tried pulling away from him but couldn't. It was easier to hug him close but the anger, the need for revenge was great. "I must kill him. Morago must die."

She felt Julius's hand caress the back of her head.

"Not tonight, mate. Not tonight."

Mate?

She was about to question his use of the word when she heard Gideon's voice. "Where is she? Where is Melena?"

"Right here, wolf. I've got her," Julius stated. It was then that she realized the fighting was over. Julius slowly released his hold somewhat until Gideon locked gazes with Julius. Both men were over six feet tall. Julius was trim, like an ultimate fighter and Gideon was thicker, more solid, like a football player. Their eyes glowed as Gideon reached his hand out for Melena to take. She looked up at Julius, his eyes glowed redder somehow, and then they went dark. Gideon pulled her to him and embraced her as he inhaled deeply against her neck.

"Thank the gods you're safe."

"Gideon! We have a situation!" someone yelled out.

It was then that she realized they had help in the fight. It was still too dark for her human eyes to see. Even though she saw more than usual, she couldn't differentiate who was who.

"What is it, Van?" Gideon asked.

"Saxton and Tango. It's not good."

"No. Oh God, no!" Melena yelled as she pulled from Gideon and ran toward the man named Van. She fell to her knees between the two men. Her only family. The tears rolled down her cheeks.

"Please help them. Please don't let them die. I need them."

She frantically looked around at the somber faces she could see. They didn't look like they were going to help but then Julius spoke.

"Take them to Dani. Dani will know what to do."

* * * *

It was incredible, but in a matter of minutes Dani showed up with another vampire named Vanderlan. He and Julius acknowledged one another with a nod as Dani gave orders. A crew of men showed up to retrieve the bodies of the fallen wolves. Melena was grateful that her men and Dani's men were all safe and alive, but her concern was for Tango and Saxton. They were carried up to the loft and placed on her bed. Her wolves weren't too thrilled but she didn't really care as she knelt at the end of the bed and stared at Tango and Saxton's bloody bodies.

"What do we do? I'll do anything you ask, Dani. I know you are a healer," Melena pleaded as tears rolled down her cheeks.

Dani stared around the room at all the men, including her own.

Julius began to walk out.

"Julius, remain. You are needed."

"No, Dani. I cannot help with this," Julius replied.

"You need to. It is the way it must be done."

"No, she deserves better and I promised," Julius stated.

"You promised who, what? What are you two talking about? Save them. Save Tango and Saxton," Melena pleaded.

"Vanderlan and my men, please leave the Dolberg men and Julius here," Dani said.

"No, mate. We cannot," Van replied.

"What do you mean you cannot?" Dani asked and Melena wondered what the heck was happening here. Saxton and Tango did not have time for some sort of argument.

"They're going to die," Melena whispered as she stared at their bodies.

"We are all part of the Secret Order. These men are our blood, our cousins, and we may be needed here. It's what the gods are telling us, Dani," Miele said.

She smiled and nodded her head. "Then remain." Dani reached her hand out to Melena.

"Take my hand, goddess."

Melena swallowed hard. So Dani knew who she was. Her men looked on with uncertainty in their eyes and Julius held her gaze. He knew. Somehow Julius knew who she really was.

"This is going to be a bit tricky, but I understand now, why this must happen like this. Melena, take Julius's hand."

"What?" Melena heard the series of voices echo at once. Julius, Gideon, Chance, Chordeo, Mano, and Edric.

"She is the mate of all of you. Julius knows this. You knew since she was a child."

Melena gasped and tried to pull away but Julius pulled her closer.

"You know what to do, Julius," Dani said.

Melena stared up into Julius's eyes. They began to glow as he held her gaze and a feeling of warmth and safety filled her soul. When he gave a small smile, she saw his sharp teeth. She wasn't afraid but instead turned on by him. His mouth descended upon her as he kissed her deeply, stroking her tongue, devouring her soft moans. She felt her arms fall to her sides as she tilted her head back and bared her neck to him.

"Do it, Julius. You must seal the bond between the seven of you. Saxton and Tango must live," Dani whispered.

Melena felt the warmth of her blood flowing through her veins. She somehow locked onto a feeling of power and a connection to Julius. She reached back and touched Saxton and Tango as Dani touched them, too. The flow of magic took away any darkness and pain. She felt it move through her blood and then darkness overtook her as feelings of peacefulness replaced the fear. Saxton and Tango would live. They would one day soon rule as leaders in the Security Ring.

* * * *

"How did you know?" Julius asked Dani as he held a sleeping Melena in his arms. Her men were there, too, as Julius placed Melena down on the empty bed. Saxton and Tango were resting in the other room.

"What is going on?" Gideon asked as he caressed Melena's hair from her cheeks.

"Your soul mate has returned to you," Dani said.

"Soul mate?" Chordeo asked.

"I promised her father that I would stay away from her," Julius said as he gently ran an index finger along Melena's chin. He was in shock at the instant bond to her. He would do anything to protect her and after feeding from her blood and feeling the magic within her, he knew she needed protection. The need for revenge on Morago was great. She was determined to bring Morago down.

"Julius, you know that the gods decide our fates. Zeikele did not know how important his daughter would be and what her role in securing were law would one day emerge. You need to forget your silly promise. He would forgive you and be honored that you were part of this," Dani said.

"Zeikele?" Gideon asked and his eyes widened, as he looked from Melena to Julius then to his brothers then back at Melena.

"Yes, Gideon. Melena is Zeikele's daughter, Kamea. She was the sole survivor ten years ago when Morago's men murdered the entire family. He thought that his men killed everyone, but Zeikele had taught his daughter well," Dani told Gideon

"She was who we scented when we arrived too late. We knew our mate had been there, but we thought her flesh was among those that were massacred," Mano whispered in shock. Now all the brothers and Julius sat around the bed.

"She is alive and well. She is the mate to all six of you. Kamea is the Goddess of the circle."

Dani smiled at their shocked expressions then began to walk toward the door.

"Protect her with all you have to offer. She seeks revenge for her family's murder and for Saxton's and Tango's injuries. She'll need all of you to keep her focused on her destiny. If she fails, if she allows revenge to rule her mind and actions, then the circle could be destroyed and were law as you know it abolished forever."

Chapter 14

She jerked upright, gasping for air. She knew she was in an unfamiliar place, yet she felt protected and warm.

"It's okay, Kamea. You are safe."

She turned toward Julius's voice and the fact that he called her by her real name. She covered her breasts with her arms, even though it was pitch black, she knew she was naked.

"Yes, we know who you are. We thought we had lost you forever," he whispered. As she began to ask who he meant by saying "we," she saw the glowing eyes illuminate the room around them. It was so very dark.

"Your men are all here. They, too, thought they had lost you forever," he said as he gently pulled her back down and against his side. He was naked, too, and her breasts pressed against his chest. She immediately felt the arousal. She clung to him as his hand roamed over her back then to her rear. A low growl filtered through the room then the bed dipped.

She glanced back over her shoulder and locked gazes with Gideon.

"You're everything to us, Melena." He kissed her softly on the lips and she felt Julius's hand tighten on her lower back.

Her mind felt fuzzy, and then she began to remember what happened.

"Saxton and Tango?"

"Are alive and well, thanks to you and Julius. They're resting at a safe location," Gideon whispered then began to stroke her shoulder with his fingers.

"They're not here? Wherever here is." She closed her eyes and allowed their touch to ease her mind.

"They're with our cousins and protected. We're at Julius's home." Gideon leaned forward and kissed her shoulder.

Her eyes shot open. "The brooch, the key to the book. We need to go back to my place and get it."

"Your place is being watched. We have men stationed there. As a matter of fact, Tango and Saxton explained to us how you obtained that brooch."

She felt like she was in trouble. "I had to break in there to get it. You see how bad Morago and the others are?"

"We nearly caught you that night." Gideon kissed her shoulder as Julius lay her back down onto the bed.

"You weren't even close," she replied with confidence and Julius chuckled.

"It's time, Melena. This is so very difficult for Julius and all of us. As Alpha males, we do not share our mates with anyone but our pack brothers. The gods have chosen Julius for reasons yet to come. We must make love to you together to not only seal our fates, but to provide our wolves comfort in knowing you are safe and secure," Gideon whispered as he rolled her to her back before taking a breast between his teeth.

"Oh, this is so crazy." She felt her legs part and Julius move between them. He caressed up her thighs and his thumbs brushed along her pussy lips. Thrusting upward, she moaned while Gideon licked her nipples and played with her breasts.

She jerked a moment as Julius used his teeth to tease and nip her clit.

"Hold her arms above her head," Julius ordered.

"Please, Julius. Let me touch you. I want to feel you when you make love to me, instead of believing that your touch is a dream."

He leaned up and stared down into her eyes. She could see him clearly.

"I have touched you before and brought you pleasure."

"You blocked my mind, controlled my reaction and fulfillment, Julius. I knew you were there at night. I felt you, smelled your scent. You let me know you were there the first time, but not the others. The other times, you just watched over me like some guardian angel." Gideon growled low and cupped her breast with one hand hard as he pulled the other nipple taut between his lips.

"Oh!"

Julius chuckled low and deep. "I am no angel, Kamea. You are mine." Julius lined his cock up with her pussy and pressed into her slowly.

Melena opened for his invasion. She needed him inside of her and she needed Gideon, too.

"We'll get to that, sweet lover. Two cocks inside of you at once will be quite pleasurable."

Gideon moved to the side as Julius made love to Melena.

She felt the deep strokes of his cock beyond her womb and straight to her heart. The connection flowed deep within her blood, it was magical and she could sense a feeling of completion just out of reach.

"I thought I lost you," he whispered as he lay over her, his hand gripping her right ass cheek as he thrust deeply in and out of her cunt. Melena wrapped her thighs tighter and dug her heels into his ass as she hugged his neck and shoulders to her tightly.

"I thought I would be lonely forever," she whispered.

"Never," both Gideon and Julius replied together, and she gasped as Julius pumped into her harder. His strokes were relentless as he thrust into her while licking and nibbling her neck. She felt the need to succumb to his command and allow Julius free access to not only her body but her soul. She tilted her head back, offering her neck as she called out his name. "Julius!"

She panted, out of breath, and grabbed at him until he bit into her neck and exploded inside of her. Melena felt her entire body convulse.

Euphoria overtook her until he kissed her mouth like some hungry lover, a man who just took his woman for the very first time.

* * * *

Gideon felt his body tighten with feelings of need so great he knew that if he didn't get inside of Melena and mark her that he would be unsettled and out of control. Julius seemed to understand as he eased out of Melena and moved to the side. He continued to caress her breasts as Gideon took position between her legs.

"So beautiful. Our goddess has returned to us."

He thrust into her, causing Melena to gasp then grab onto his wrists. She thrust upward, meeting his strokes with urgency like his own. With every stroke into her, his love and desire grew stronger. Even as Julius took her mouth with his own and swallowed her moans of pleasure, Gideon felt the deep connection grow between the three of them. As the bed dipped, he knew that Mano had joined them.

"Sweet woman, I need you," Mano whispered and Julius released her lips and trailed fingers along her breast as Mano fisted his cock next to her mouth. Their lovely goddess knew what her mate wanted as she licked her lips then opened for him, taking Mano's cock.

"Oh yeah, so good," Mano said as he caressed her hair and thrust slowly into her mouth.

The sight was too much for Gideon. He increased his strokes as he watched Melena suck his brother's cock.

"So fucking hot and sexy," he whispered as he ran his fingers up her chest and over her breasts to her throat. She tilted up and moaned against Mano.

"Incredible." Julius nipped her nipple. Gideon felt his body tighten and he thrust into Melena, causing her to release Mano's cock.

"Oh!" she screamed as she convulsed beneath him. Gideon exploded inside of her as he bit into her shoulder, sealing the bond.

The room erupted in an invisible energy that consumed them all. Gideon moved from between her legs and Mano flipped Melena to her belly, pulled her up on all fours, and plunged into her from behind.

She screamed at the invasion then thrust her ass backward.

"Fuck, my wolf is out of control. I need to come inside of you. I need to claim you as mine, woman. I thought I would never know you, mate. I thought the opportunity was lost and that the gods had decided we would be alone with no mate forever. I need you." Mano grunted as he thrust again and again.

The bed dipped and Chordeo was there kissing Melena on the mouth before he fisted his cock as he stood up on his knees. Their voracious woman opened wide and took Chordeo's cock into her mouth. She looked incredible.

* * * *

Chance watched his brothers and Julius make love to their mate. He paced the edge of the bed, wanting, needing to claim her next. Mano roared as he exploded inside of her then bit into her shoulder marking her.

Their sweet, sexy goddess, moaned with pleasure and as she gazed at him, she looked like a seductress. Wet lips, glossy green eyes, love marks along her neck and chest. She appeared edible to Chance.

Chordeo moved in behind her and thrust into her immediately. She moaned and thrust backward against him.

Chance was utterly turned on by the way Chordeo's large hands grasped Melena's hips. They were huge and dominating. Melena didn't seem weak or unable to keep up with some voracious, wild men. Instead she looked up with confidence and sexual drive that magically encased the room.

Chance took his position by her mouth. He needed to feel her touch, her lips, some part of her before his wolf lost control. He stroked his long, hard cock against her cheek as she panted for breath.

"I don't know if I can."

"You can and you will. You're the mate to five Alpha wolves and a vampire," Julius teased then stroked her ass with his fingers. She moaned and Chordeo gripped her hips tighter and exploded inside of her. He bit into her shoulder then licked the wound as he laid his cheek on her shoulder.

"Perfection." He kissed her cheek.

Chance rolled her to her back and held her hands above her head as he straddled her. She held his gaze and smiled.

"You little minx. You can handle all of us, like a good Alpha female that you are."

He thrust into her slowly as their fingers entwined.

Chance rocked his hips against Melena's. The louder she moaned the deeper he thrust into her.

They locked gazes, and he knew in that moment that they were sealing their bonds as mates and lovers. This was only the beginning of their happiness. She would always be part of him and his brothers. They were her protectors, her lovers, her everything for eternity.

"Oh, Chance. My legs are shaking."

He chuckled.

"They'll get used to it, every time we all take you like this. Always like this, sweet Melena." Chance lifted her thighs over his thighs, smoothed his palms underneath her ass, and parted the cheeks as he plunged deeper into her pussy. With every deep stroke and warm breath of Melena's against his chest, his wolf settled down and knew the bond was taking. She began to moan louder and then she bit gently against his neck. He lost control as he felt his body lose the battle to take more of Melena and he exploded inside of her. Leaning down, he bit into her shoulder and marked her like his brothers had then kissed her mouth and hugged her to him.

* * * *

Edric was breathing heavy. He couldn't wait. He needed her so badly his wolf let out a low growl. He stood at the edge of the bed, trying to catch his breath. Melena rolled from Chance's arms and stared at him.

"Come to me," she whispered. He leaped onto the bed right between her legs.

She squealed and he laughed as he hugged her to him.

"The best for last, sweetheart." She smiled then opened wide as he slowly pushed his cock into her cunt. She felt slick and warm and oh, so very good, instantly easing the anxiety his wolf had felt.

He caressed her curves, absorbed the calmness around the room as his brothers and Julius watched in ease.

Edric moved his fingers through her long brown hair and held her face between his hands as he sat up. Her thighs were over his thighs and he could feel her juices drip between them.

"So sexy and wet. Your body knows that you belong to us. You feel it don't you, baby?"

"Yes, Edric. I want more. I want you all everywhere."

He adjusted his body and flipped Melena onto her belly shocking her. She gasped as she turned and a moment later he was back inside of her, pumping his hips into her pussy from behind.

"Let's see how this feels."

He ran a finger from her pussy to her ass with one hand while he cupped her breast with the other. Melena moaned as he pressed his finger through the tight rings and into her ass.

"Oh!" She moaned then pushed back against his finger and it was way out of control. He increased his thrusts and pulled on her breast. He felt the feeling of satisfaction just out of reach as he thrust his cock into her pussy and his finger into her ass as he pulled on her breasts. He inhaled deeply, instantly smelling the aroma of Melena's cream and he needed more. He let go of her breast and wrapped an arm tightly around her midsection as he pulled back and shoved his cock into her deeply. He roared as he bit into her shoulder, marking her like his brothers had, before he felt her go limp in his arms.

"Ours, forever."

Chapter 15

"What would you like to do? Fight one another? I am just as shocked as you are, Gideon," Julius stated firmly as Gideon paced in front of him.

Gideon ran his fingers through his hair.

"You knew she was your mate the first time you saw her at the gala."

"I knew she was my intended mate when she was a child, living in Hawaii with her family."

Gideon widened his eyes.

"How can that be?"

"Easy. I was a friend of Zeikele, her father. I was present in the meeting where he declared having information on certain packs forming armies to strengthen their positions. He was a forceful and very intelligent wolf. He loved his family dearly." Julius walked over toward the wall by the fake window. Outside it was daylight, but he was floors below his estate in a makeshift home of darkness. He should be sleeping, but he yearned for his mate. This was one negative that would surely take a toll on Melena.

"I saw Melena when she was born. I visited the house often, but it wasn't until she turned eleven that I realized she was of some greater importance to me than Zeikele's daughter. He noticed how I would watch her and he made me swear that I would stay away from her. He didn't want his only daughter mated to a vampire and stuck living for eternity. He didn't even want people to know of her existence."

"He was trying to protect her from her destiny. It explains why he trained her the way he did," Gideon stated.

"It was that training that saved her life. I don't know the details of her experience, but having the ability to read her thoughts, I know she seeks revenge on Morago. I know she saw her family massacred."

"My brothers and I entered the Mahalan home after the attack. Lord Crespin sent us at the time, but we were too late. The one thing about what we felt and saw that will always remain in our minds was her scent. We knew our mate was present, but with all that blood and torn flesh, we assumed she had been killed."

"You've all lived your life as I have. A mate not meant to be ours and one taken from us because of the betrayal and criminal mind of killers. The gods call us to Melena now for good reason. She is in danger. As soon as Morago realizes that Zeikele's daughter is alive, he will hunt her down."

"Then we must put our annoyance with this situation behind us, wolf. An ultimate power has made this decision and we must abide."

"That is not going to be so easy, Julius."

"Tell me about it. I have never broken a promise and I have never shared a woman with anyone, never mind wolves."

Gideon smirked.

"We will survive as long as we put Melena first."

"Agreed."

* * * *

Melena was fixing Saxton's pillow behind his head as he sat on the couch, and then she helped to put Tango's feet up. Around the room her wolves sat making low growling noises. She turned to them.

"Cut it out. They need coddling. They nearly died."

Saxton held her hand and sniffed her.

"A lot happened while we slept."

She blushed.

"I'd say so."

"Why haven't any of you marked her?" he asked.

Gideon now entered the room. Julius remained downstairs since it was daylight.

"What do you mean?" he asked as he pulled Melena closer to him. He wrapped his arms around her from behind and nuzzled her neck. He loved that she smelled of him and his brothers. The bond was taking. His wolf was a bit upset at the traces of Vampire intertwined, but he supposed they had no choice but to get used to it.

"She is not marked. There are no bites," Tango added.

Gideon scrunched his eyes and Melena reached up to touch where the men had bitten her. She knew the purpose. In marking her, they let every wolf know that she was taken and mated to them. She felt the smooth skin.

"They're gone," Gideon said.

Melena was feeling different all morning. She couldn't quite place her finger on the reason why, but she knew things were different. She blamed it on having sex with five wolves and a vampire, but something told her it was more.

She remembered hitting the pavement during the battle outside their home. She had cut her elbow and upper arm badly. Pulling from Gideon's embrace she looked at her arm. Nothing.

"What is it?" Chance asked her.

"I know I cut my arm last night. I felt the stinging sensation and saw the blood. I was so worried about Tango and Saxton that I didn't remember until now."

"What could it mean?" Chordeo asked.

"She has magic flowing through her," Cullen said as he entered the room. He was Julius's friend and he maintained the house.

"What do you mean, Cullen?" Chordeo asked him.

"Kamea is a goddess of Polynesian decent. It is a rare breed of wolf but important to the sanctity of the circle. Her ancestors helped to establish the circle of elders many moons ago."

"I thought the Goddess of the circle was a legend?" Mano asked.

"Yeah, someone the elders made up to place fear into the children so they followed wolf law and didn't go rogue," Edric said.

"Afraid not," Melena replied sarcastically then looked at Cullen.

He squinted his eyes at her. "You did not tell them?"

She shook her head.

"Tell us what?" Gideon asked.

"I am this Goddess of the circle as you know. However, I also have the power to decide who remains as circle members and who needs to step down. I have been working on creating the Security Ring to ensure that once the circle of elders is in place, that they will be safe and secure."

The men appeared shocked but then Gideon appeared upset.

"They'll want to kill her or make her help them to overtake the circle."

"Exactly. That is why you, your brothers, and Julius need to protect her. At any moment the magic that has sealed her identity will be released. She will no longer be able to hide from the enemy. In fact, when these men realize that Zeikele's daughter Kamea is alive and well, they will want to possess her for her land and her bloodline. There are only a few living relatives of hers and they have been placed under a protective spell by the gods."

"Wonderful," Chordeo replied.

"This could work well actually," Melena said as she stood by the window and looked out. She wanted to destroy the bad guys and secure the circle. Perhaps making her presence known would pull these creeps out of the woodwork.

"What crazy ideas are you formulating, Melena?" Gideon asked.

"Oh, just thinking that perhaps if Morago, Filletto, and the count knew that I was a Mahalan, then maybe they would let me in on their plans to destroy the circle, and we could stop them."

"Absolutely not. They would finish the job and kill you," Chance stated firmly and the others added their concerns.

Or perhaps, he would try to mate you himself and take over everything that belongs to the Mahalan name," Edric added with his arms crossed as he glared at Melena. He looked her body over and she seemed to understand his line of thinking.

"Morago is going down, whether you all are willing to help me or not. Let's get things moving. I have made a decision on the last two members of the Security Ring. I think seven is sufficient. If necessary, I can always appoint more in the future."

"What about Donovan?" Mano asked.

"Dani said that he is all clear. Mercer was being manipulated and threatened by the count. Donovan still has my vote."

"And the last two?" Mano asked.

"Their identities will remain hidden for now. Let's see if we can let out the information that Kamea Mahalan is indeed alive."

* * * *

Mano sat in the chair watching Melena as she worked. She was lovelier than any woman he had ever seen. Did he think that because she was his mate, or was it because she was a Polynesian goddess? He wasn't certain, but he did feel differently inside. His wolf wasn't quite at peace. It was on guard, wanting to protect what was his. He had thought his mate was gone forever. He never expected for her to emerge from the dead, but Melena did, as far as he was concerned. She had been taken away from him, by evil, disloyal wolves who deserved to suffer. He thanked the gods as he inhaled, her scent calming his wolf and enticing it at the same time. She looked up toward him and smiled.

"You're staring at me again, Mano. I can't possibly concentrate when you do that."

He stood up and walked closer to her. Leaning down, he whispered in her ear as he absorbed her scent.

"You are exquisite, and I can't keep my eyes off of you."

She tilted her head up and kissed his lips. That kiss grew deeper and soon he was kneeling on the floor between her legs and embracing her.

She opened for him, giving his hands access to her thighs as he caressed under her skirt. They battled for control over the kiss until they were both breathing heavy.

"I want you."

"I want you, too, but anyone could walk in, including Cullen."

"I don't really care and if Cullen has any sense at all, he would knock before he enters."

Mano pulled her hips toward him causing her to fall backward and spread her thighs wider.

He made quick use of his fingers, divesting her of her panties before pressing fingers to her pussy.

"Oh, Mano." She held on to the arms of the chair and thrust her hips against his fingers.

"You're wet and ready for me, mate."

"Always."

She nodded her head and he smiled as he undid his pants then lifted her up off of the chair. He sat down in it, and she straddled his waist, taking his cock between her wet folds as she gasped.

"Fuck yeah. Ride me, Melena. Show me how turned on you are."

She lifted then lowered her pussy in slow even strokes. He used his large hands to squeeze her ass and spread the cheeks. Stroking fingers back and forth across the tight bud seemed to make her move faster and ride his cock with vigor. The sounds of her moans of pleasure fed his wolf's ego and he wanted every part of her. All of her forever.

It was torture to not touch every inch of her as he undid the buttons on her blouse and played with her breasts. He leaned forward to lick the tip and taste her delicious skin.

"Oh, that feels so nice."

"Ride him."

Mano smiled as Melena gasped in shock as Chordeo joined them in the room. She hadn't heard the door open or noticed his entry but now Chordeo was behind her and Mano knew what he had in mind.

"I want you, too. Will you let me?"

"Oh God, yes. Please, I feel so tight and needy."

"Did you find lube? Don't hurt her when you fuck her ass," Mano said to Chordeo through their mind link.

"My ass? Oh my God, this is crazy. Yes, do it, please."

Mano grabbed her face between his hands.

"You heard us?"

She nodded her head as Chordeo squeezed some lube onto his fingers.

"What?" she asked in surprise.

"You heard me talking to Chordeo through our mind link. You can hear our thoughts?"

"Holy crap, yes. Yes, I thought you spoke aloud. Oh my God." Melena was so surprised and the excitement in her voice, in her facial expression, brought Mano such joy.

Mano smiled as he pulled her down closer so he could kiss her deeply.

He felt her body jerk then tighten and he knew that his brother was pushing his fingers into her ass and getting her ready for his cock.

He released her lips.

"Oh God, Mano, it burns," she said then began to ride Mano faster. Up and down, she sped up until Chordeo pulled his fingers from her ass.

"I want in, baby. You look so fucking beautiful."

Mano held her gaze as Chordeo gently pushed her lower.

"Nice and easy, baby. Let him in and we'll both make love to you together," Mano whispered and she hugged him as she breathed softly against his shoulder and ear.

"Fuck, she's tight and hot. Oh yeah, baby, you make me so happy," Chordeo said. Then Mano heard her gasp and he knew that Chordeo was all the way in.

"Nice and slow. Lift up, so I can see these pretty plump breasts of yours, baby."

She slowly rose, eyes closed and then Mano lifted her up then pressed her back down. Chordeo pulled back then slowly pressed in. They moved slowly until Melena adjusted to the fact that two men had their cocks deep inside of her. She gripped Mano's shoulders. He felt her nails.

"Easy, baby, you're doing so good. You feel so fucking amazing."

"I need you two to move. It's so crazy but I need more. Please give it to me harder."

Mano smiled then winked over her shoulder at Chordeo.

They began to increase their thrusts until neither one of them could control their desire to claim her like this. She was their mate, their lover, their goddess, and they needed to fulfill the need burning inside of them.

Melena moaned and thrust between them until finally their strokes became wild and uneven and she screamed her release. Mano and Chordeo followed suit.

"Ours. Always and forever."

* * * *

Dani and her men joined Melena, Edric, Chance, and Gideon in the study. In their investigation they helped to interrogate the wolves who attacked them at the apartment complex and ultimately figured out what the secret society was.

"It appears that this information you found out about Melena, at the warehouse was a secret meeting of the TAMW. These men that we questioned said it was an organization created by Morago to ultimately build an army of were against the circle," Dani said.

"Son of a bitch," Gideon stated.

"The letters stand for Tactical Assault, Modern Were. According to these men who ratted Morago out, TAMW was established ten years ago then put on hold when the government tried to intervene in the attack on a member of the circle, Lord Crespin. In doing so, Morago retaliated in anger and went after the Mahalan family," Van told them. Everyone looked at Melena.

"I knew that he was responsible. If he had killed me along with the rest of my family, the circle would be in jeopardy," Melena said.

"With this information and what we are learning from these rogue wolves who turned, we already informed the higher-ups and alerts have been sent out to all elders of the circle," Miele said.

"Are you tracking Morago?" Melena asked.

"Yes. He is under surveillance now. We have men collecting the evidence, securing the testimonies of witnesses so we can bring Morago, Filletto, and the count before the elders for their punishments," Dani stated.

"They will live?"

Everyone looked at her and she knew they could see her anger and dissatisfaction.

"They have the final say, Melena. But now you can complete your recommendation for the Security Ring and place those members into their positions. The circle will be safe because of you," Van added.

"What can we do to assist in getting this arrest moving? I want Melena safe, and until Morago, Filletto, and the count are behind bars, that's not going to happen. He could still get his hands on the Book of the Founding Fathers," Edric stated.

"You and Chance can assist us. Melena has placed the key to the book in a secure location. I believe Julius is aware of it," Miele said as Gideon took Melena's hand.

"No one but Melena and her mates should know the location of that key," Gideon stated.

"I agree. The fewer, the better," Van said.

"I personally, would prefer Morago, the count, and Filletto to be punished for their crimes before the circle of elders and the new Security Ring. It will send a clear message that the new command in the circle of elders are stronger than ever," Melena added.

"With your assistance, Melena, that is becoming a reality. Let us help to ensure these wolves are captured so you can move on with your new role as Goddess of the circle and mate," Van stated.

She smiled as they all began to exit the room.

She closed her eyes and immediately she heard Julius's voice. She smiled.

"Come to me, goddess, and bring Gideon."

"Where is the key?" Gideon asked her.

"The key is embedded in the brooch," Melena whispered.

She looked up at Gideon, but he turned, pulling her along with him then down the hallway to the basement door. He entered the codes that Julius obviously told him then paused at the main door.

Gideon pulled Melena into his arms.

"You are so amazing. I can't wait to make love to you."

He kissed her deeply then released her lips as they entered the darkness.

Melena paused as Gideon closed the door. He walked toward the side and lit the lantern.

Julius was sitting up on the bed, a black silk sheet only covered him from the waist down.

She felt the buttons of her blouse begin to pop off and then her blouse flew off, her skirt next and she was left in her skimpy bra and panties.

"Julius!" she reprimanded him, and Gideon chuckled.

She glanced at Gideon who now stood completely naked and holding a tube of lube. He tapped it against his palm.

"Someone told me you like the idea of a cock in your ass."

She lowered her eyes then licked her lips before nibbling her bottom lip.

"Kamea." Julius said her name as her arms fell to her sides and her bra slipped from her body. The panties tore from her skin as she gasped in shock.

"That is so fucking cool," Gideon said.

In a flash she was on the bed, completely naked and spread wide for their pleasure.

* * * *

He could feel her heart beat and her blood pump through her veins. It fed his hunger for her. Julius knew she was already a part of him just as Gideon and his brothers were, too. He spread her thighs wider as Gideon held both her wrists in one hand above her head.

"She is perfect." Gideon licked across her right nipple.

"I dreamed of her and of taking her with you, Gideon." Julius licked her pussy before plunging his tongue into her.

Melena moaned as she turned her head side to side.

Julius felt so needy and greedy for a taste of her cream. He nipped her clitoris, and used his powers to keep her thighs spread wide.

Running his hands up and down her inner thighs he absorbed her scent, her moans of pleasure.

Glancing up at her face, he held her green eyes, saw her chest heaving up and down, and he bared his fangs.

"Mine." He bit into her inner groin making Melena scream her release. Her scent filled the air and Julius knew that the wolf needed her, too.

He lowered over her body, took her mouth, and ravished her.

Rolling him to his back, she immediately straddled him, taking his cock into her wet pussy.

"Oh, Julius!" she moaned then began to ride him.

Gideon moved behind her, caressed her shoulders and sucked along her neck.

"You smell amazing. I can't wait to be inside of you, mate." He gently ran his teeth along her neck and Julius thrust upward. She gripped his shoulders and eased her body lower in anticipation for Gideon's attack.

Up and down, back and forth, she rode Julius until Gideon pressed the lube to her ass.

"Oh, Gideon. Oh God, I can't believe I feel like this. Get inside of me, Gideon. Please," she begged, sounding desperate, and Julius chuckled. He gripped her hair and pulled her lower.

"Such a demanding little goddess."

"Here I come, baby," Gideon whispered then grabbed onto her shoulders from behind and thrust into her in one smooth stroke.

"Oh!" she screamed and Gideon pulled back then shoved back into her.

Together Julius and Gideon took turns bringing her pleasure and satisfying their need to mate and claim. Julius could read her mind. She was happy, content but about to pass out from the powerful sex.

"Come now, Melena, and then we will follow," Julius ordered. She shook and screamed her release. Gideon followed, biting into her shoulder as Julius did the same. He exploded then bit into her flesh, feeding on her blood and connecting with Gideon. Something amazing happened. The bond, the visions overtook Julius as Melena passed out.

"Did you feel that?" Julius asked Gideon.

"Not only did I feel it, but I saw images in my head."

Gideon eased out of Melena and grabbed his pants, pulling them on before lying on the bed next to Melena.

"We must protect her from harm. She still seeks revenge on Morago."

"I know, Julius, and I can't blame her one bit. She lost everything because of him."

"Then we must do what we can to bring her family justice. The gods have spoken."

Chapter 16

"Where is Melena now?" Mano asked Gideon and Julius as they entered the meeting room.

"She is resting. Chance and Edric are with her," Gideon said then smiled at his brother.

"She is amazing. To think that all this time she was still alive and we thought our mate was dead. Thank the gods she is so strong," Mano stated.

"Our Polynesian goddess packs a hell of a punch. I don't think I'll ever be the same man or wolf again," Chordeo admitted and they all nodded their heads.

"So what did I miss?" Julius asked. Mano and Chordeo filled him in on the investigation.

"There's one piece missing from this secret plan of Morago's to overthrow the circle."

"What's that, Julius?" Van asked.

"Morago has been searching for treasures and valuable jewels. It's how I found out about him trying to claim the pendant of light."

"The pendant of light?" Van asked.

"Yes, it is a valuable pendant more in meaning than monetary value, to vampires. It was lost during the great battle of wizards. My ancestors held the pendant in their home. During the war, the wizards went crazy and began to destroy everything in their path until the Goddess of light intervened. The pendant was lost until Morago came upon it in a slew of other jewels he found while digging in the Netherlands. The count paid Morago for the pendant but it was mine. That night at the gala I was trying to get it back from him."

"That explains what Melena said about you being there and being angry with the count. But all of this just means that Morago was trying to gain funds for his venture in taking over the circle," Gideon said.

"Perhaps not. While we searched Morago's offices, we came upon a safe and inside were various stories from the elders. They had to do with the establishment of the circle," Miele told them.

"Well, if he wanted to take over the circle, perhaps Morago was looking over the protocol," Chordeo suggested.

"No one but the Founding Fathers' family and the Goddess of the circle can reestablish it," Dani added.

"Maybe Morago is planning on reestablishing his family claim to the original throne of were."

They all turned toward the doorway as the vampire Vanderlan entered.

"Vanderlan, what are you talking about?"

"Randolph, Bently, Baher, and I had a little discussion with Warnerbe Pierce. It seems he's been getting paid to do a lot of illegal work for Morago. He believes that Morago has knowledge of the location of the Book of the Founding Fathers. He thinks that he can gain power by possessing it and using the Pendant of Light to see the contents."

"Can he do that, Julius? Is that how the pendant works?" Miele asked.

"So if Morago kills the elders of the circle and holds possession of the book, then he automatically rules? I don't think it works that way," Van replied.

"I am not certain if the Pendant of Light can be used to reveal the contents of the book. I thought the key and brooch that Kamea has is the only way," Julius said.

Everyone was quiet a moment. They were all uneasy.

"Why don't we just arrest him now and end all this bullshit?" Gideon asked.

Vanderlan cleared his throat.

"Morago has disappeared," Vanderlan said, and the room fell silent.

"I'm not willing to take the chance that possessing the Book of the Founding Fathers will give Morago power to rule. We should call Samantha," Van suggested.

"I'm on it now," Dani said then left the room.

* * * *

Melena washed her hair after soaping up her body. She sensed Edric and Chance undressing and smiled to herself.

"I thought you two were never going to join me," she teased.

Her own words shocked her. Never would she think she'd be so brazen with lovers. Then again, never had she thought about having more than one lover.

There was this constant urge, an ache to have them each near her.

"We feel it, too, Melena. It's part of the mating process," Edric said as he pulled her into his arms and kissed her.

She tried her hardest to wrap her arms around his upper shoulders, but it was no use. He was too big. Edric seemed to be the most easygoing of the brothers. But he was just as intimidating in appearance and size. He wore his black hair very short and was built with ridges of muscles and appeared strong as an ox.

She felt Edric lift her up, and instinctively she straddled his waist and allowed him access to her body. She loved how her inner thighs and pussy felt, flush against his washboard stomach. It gave her the chills, aroused her senses, and made her mind think of nothing but his thick cock filling her.

"As you wish, sweet goddess," he whispered and she knew he heard her thoughts as she smiled and held his gaze.

He licked across her lower lip then pulled it into his mouth before plunging his tongue inside. It became a tiny battle to control the kiss as he eased his cock between her wet folds. Thrusting into her, she moaned with satisfaction. It seemed a new hunger for her mates' cocks was growing deeper and deeper.

"I can take care of that itch for you and then Chance will help, too."

Edric's fingers stroked over her puckered hole and she tightened her hold on his waist. In and out he thrust his hips. His cock rubbed back and forth over her inner muscles. It was crazy, but she felt the itch intensify as she ground her hips harder against his strokes.

"You have a great ass, Melena. I love being inside of you," Edric told her.

"I love having you inside of me," she replied between panting, as she held on to his shoulders. Edric was so easygoing. He appeared so military-like and lethal.

She couldn't resist pushing her fingers through his hair, or caressing his firm, muscular cheeks. He was so sexy her belly quivered.

He pressed her body against the tiled wall then grabbed hold of her ass cheeks. Spreading them as he tilted then stroked her cunt had her gasping for breath. She held on to him and rode out each wave of pleasure until Edric came inside of her. He bit into her shoulder then licked and sucked the wound until he was certain she was okay.

"My turn," Chance said as Edric kissed her lips then turned her around to face Chance. Chance pulled her into his arms and hugged her tight.

Chance pressed her back against the wall as she straddled his waist. He cupped her face between his hands and stared down into her eyes as the water cascaded over her breasts and between them.

"We thought we had lost you forever. To know that you survived what you did, escaped, and now are part of us is a dream, a miracle come true."

She felt the tears in her eyes and the depth of his emotions.

As charming, charismatic, and flirtatious as Chance always seemed to be, his revelation of emotions here with her now made the bond between them grow stronger. He was already such a large part of her she wondered how she'd even survived this long without her mates.

He leaned forward and kissed her softly on the lips. Feeling needy, she reached down and took his cock between her fingers to align with her pussy.

He released her lips and stared at her.

"Make love to me, Chance."

"As you wish, goddess." He lowered his hips and slowly pushed into her. She gripped his shoulders and he pulled her hands up and above her head. Their foreheads touched as he pulled back then thrust forward. She dug her heels into his waist to hold on as he made love to her in slow, even strokes.

"Please, Chance. Please move faster, harder. I need so much."

His hands moved down her inner arms, over her breasts, causing tiny goose bumps to scatter over her skin and then to her hips. He pulled out then thrust slowly into her. She wanted to beg him for more, to go harder, faster but then he reached down, spread her ass cheeks and thrust so deeply into her that she lost her breath. Digging her fingernails into his shoulders seemed to egg him on as Chance pumped faster, deeper until they both exploded together. Biting into her shoulder, he growled and she moaned as they held one another close until Chance was ready to release her.

* * * *

"They're searching for you, Morago. They know about the book and your plan," Lance, Filletto's main wolf, informed him over the phone.

"I don't really care. Everything I have worked for has been destroyed."

"Did you hear the latest? That brunette that was with Xavier Dolberg and his nephews is Zeikele's daughter."

"What?"

"Yes, it was confirmed. She survived the attacked ten years ago. Tango and Saxton have been her guards and protectors."

"What does it matter that she lives?"

"She owns the land and estate in Hawaii. The same location that you tried taking over and now believe treasures to be buried on."

"Son of a bitch. She'll get everything. She'll be wealthy beyond any power including the circle."

"Word is, she's part of securing the circle members. It seems she is taking over her father's role as a protector and investigator."

"Where is she now?"

"Probably with her mates."

"Mates? Who, the Dolberg Pack?"

"And Julius Kordosky."

"No. It can't be."

"It is. So I think your fight is over. You've lost, Morago. Disappear and never return."

Morago hung up the phone and stared out at the city buildings. He was boarding a plane and heading to Hawaii in a day. He needed to get Kamea and bring her with him.

He looked at the treasures he had packed in the large black suitcase. Jewels, the Pendant of Light, which he still thought was meaningful in some way to the circle, not just the vampire world. Then he looked at the book. It was not the Book of the Founding Fathers, but instead the diary of Dr. Henry Lesting.

Coriano Morago took it into his hands and flipped through the pages. There were detailed stories of the doctor's interviews with fairies and other mystical creatures about other realms. There were experiments not fully developed, but marked for future attempts. The one that caught Morago's interest was the one about altering one's intended mate and forcing a bond. Then there was the experiment about creating a breed of wolf superior in nature to any other wolf forms. Like guards of the ever world, these wolves would be huge, powerful and evil, but most importantly, loyal to their creator. This was what Morago hoped to achieve. But now it seemed too late.

He closed the book, placed it into a special velvet bag and decided who would be the best person and most loyal wolf to secure the book while he took some time away to evade capture.

He thought about it and it hit him. His cousin, Paul of the Tennessee Morago Pack. They were a wild bunch of men. Paul liked to keep to himself and remained sort of rogue, just like Coriano Morago. He would take care of this before he left for his trip.

He'd wasted so many years seeking this power. He killed, he stole, and he gave up his family heritage to achieve greatness. Possessing the book and killing the elders would have brought him success.

The anger and hatred filled him to his core.

She must die.

In an instant, Coriano Morago heard the alerts. Someone was breaking into the penthouse. They were coming for him. He grabbed his other suitcase, leaving the jewels behind but not the book. It was more important to get the book to his cousin than anything else. He ran to the hidden door behind the bookcase. It closed as the sound of men yelling filled his penthouse suite.

He headed down the stairs and private elevator. It had been ingenious to make such an escape route when he built this building. It led to a tunnel and private garage. He would wait to make his escape.

The urge to seek revenge and to secure power as he evaded capture was pushing his wolf to make a drastic decision. How could he get to Kamea with her heavy security? Could he get to her and take her with him to Hawaii?

He needed time to think, to plan. Right now, getting the book to Paul was crucial. He decided to get to safety then scan the book and forward the copy to his cousin. In the interim, the book would be with him at all times. Afterward, he would make his next strategic move.

Chapter 17

Melena looked at the items that were taken from Morago's place. She couldn't believe the things that were found in Coriano Morago's penthouse. Julius was thrilled to get the Pendant of Light back. He placed it in safekeeping in his safe at home along with the Mahalan brooch. It was amazing how the information just came to her in regards to the key's whereabouts. She assumed it had something to do with the magic surrounding her that Saxton and Tango mentioned.

Dani felt that Melena should be the one to secure the items.

When she looked at a special box, locked with no key hole she held it in her hand and turned it around. "How odd."

"What is it, Melena?" Edric asked as he joined her in the room.

"I don't know. There is something about this box. I'm not sure what it is, Edric, but it means something important. I just know it."

"What's going on?" Gideon asked as he walked into the room next, followed by Julius, Mano, Chance, and Chordeo. They had packed their bags and were taking her to her home in Hawaii. She desperately wanted to go there, even though Morago had disappeared.

"She found this box with no lock or key to open it," Edric said.

She showed it to the others.

"That's strange. Maybe it's empty?" Chance added. She shook her head. Melena knew it wasn't empty and then a thought came to her mind.

Ask the gods and they will guide you.

She looked at her men and they smiled. She knew they heard the voice in her head.

She closed her eyes and held the small box to her chest.

The magical feeling encased her entire body. She had the vision flow through her mind, taking her on a journey about the box and its contents. There were three special rings inside of the box. These rings represented three special goddesses who would help to establish a royal hierarchy alongside her and above the circle. They would stand side by side with the gods that ruled above all were, fairies, and creatures of other realms. Melena was shocked as the magic that had protected her thus far lifted from her body. She clutched the box tighter and knew that there was more to come. There would be battles ahead of her and her men. Her destiny now lay in securing these three women who would wear the rings and stand by her side to protect and unite the bonds of all mystical creatures.

She heard her name being called by her men. She realized that they had been blocked from viewing what she had just seen. She had new insight, felt the power within her surround her, and knew that it would always be there to guide her.

Her eyes fluttered open. All six of her mates held angry expressions and she smiled, which only seemed to anger them more.

"This box remains with me. The others go into the vault at Julius's home."

Chance grabbed her arm and turned her toward him. "You blocked us out. What happened?"

She caressed his arm as she smiled up at him.

Chance wasn't used to being kept out of the picture. He wanted to protect her at all times and she knew and understood his personality so well now. The way his dimple was more pronounced when he smiled and the way his eyes darkened when aroused. She was learning about each of her men thoroughly.

"The gods have spoken again to me, Chance. We must secure the contents of this special box. We must ensure that we remain together as one unit, one power to fight what has yet to come. I love you all so much and I know that I am no longer alone and will need you. All of you," she said as she looked at her men.

"And we will need you, too, goddess. We are here to protect and serve." Julius bowed his head before he wrapped his arm around her waist and pulled her to him. He caressed the hair from her cheeks and stared down into her eyes.

"You must learn that you are not always in charge and are the mate to six Alpha men. I'd say you need some more instruction in submission. How about you, guys?" he asked the others as he held her gaze.

Melena pretended concern but inside her belly did a series of flips and her pussy clenched with need for her men.

"Please be gentle." She threw a hand over her eyes as she closed them and bared her neck to her Alpha wolf.

"Gentle is overrated," Gideon stated as he began to undress. The others followed as Julius carried her over to the long couch, removing her clothing with his mind, which she was totally getting used to.

She stared at them, her six Alpha men, and immediately forgot any feelings or memories of ever being alone in this world. Her reservations about the future and what obstacle might try to destroy their bond and love diminished with their kisses, their acts of love that brought her pleasure.

Now naked and fully exposed to her six sexy men, she opened her thighs, placed one arm above her head, and used her other hand and fingers to stroke her own pussy as they watched with hunger.

"I need so badly. Can you help me please?" she teased, and Julius shocked her by pulling her thighs toward his naked body so that her ass hung off of the couch and he stared at her with glowing red eyes.

"It seems we are all very hungry, mate. I don't think we'll be making our flight this evening." He thrust into her making her gasp as Gideon grabbed hold of her hands and clasped them with his fingers.

"Wolves and vampires can make love for days."

"Oh," she moaned as Julius stroked his cock deeper, harder into her.

"Yes, that's right, mate. We've got fantasies and plans for you," Chance said, and when she looked at him, he was naked and held a tube of lube in his hands.

Gideon sat down beside her and caressed her breasts. She closed her eyes and relished in their touch until Julius pulled out of her, lifted her by her waist, turned her around, and made her straddle Gideon. Gideon immediately thrust upward into her cunt making her scream his name. Melena held on to his shoulders and rode him hard and fast until he dipped his body lower, making her lose her balance.

She immediately felt Julius's hands steadying her. A quick glance over her shoulder and Chance threw the tube at Julius. She felt the cool liquid against her puckered hole and instinctually pushed back against Julius's fingers.

Gideon latched onto her breast and she squealed from the sudden bite.

Her pussy dripped and he thrust upward as Julius pushed his cock through the tight rings of her ass.

Melena felt so out of control and needy.

"Yes, yes, like that, Julius. Harder," she demanded.

Then Julius and Gideon began a sequence of hard, fast strokes as Melena felt her body erupt in pleasure. She could sense her teeth elongating, her fingernails sharpening, and a growl erupting from her throat. As she exploded along with Julius and Gideon, she bit into Gideon's neck and fed from his blood as Julius bit into her neck and fed from her. Gideon roared as he shoved upward with his cock.

* * * *

As they caught their breath and recovered, Julius was in shock. He looked at Gideon's neck and Melena had definitely bit the wolf and sealed the wound.

"Gideon?" He said his name and Gideon smiled, eyes closed and appearing very content. Julius chuckled as Melena pulled back.

"Holy crap," she whispered and Julius smiled. He stared into her green, glowing eyes, uncertain what exactly she was. Was she wolf, was she vampire, or perhaps a bit of both? There was something more.

"We need her now," Edric interrupted and Julius looked at him, Chance, Mano, and Chordeo. He nodded his head and kissed Melena before pulling from her ass.

Gideon held her in place then opened his eyes to look at her.

"Something amazing just happened."

"I know. I need to feed from the others. I need to bite them as they come inside of me. We all need to share the power, strength, and connection. It will help in the battles that lie ahead," Melena said as Chordeo lifted up off of Gideon and pulled her against his chest.

Julius smiled then sat back in a chair and watched his mate make love to her other mates and empower all of them beyond any fantasy story any of them had ever heard of.

* * * *

Chordeo wasted no time. He pressed Melena against the wall and entered her in one, smooth thrust. She grabbed onto his arms and accepted his attack. And it was an attack. Their mate had glowing green eyes and long sharp fangs and nails that pressed into his skin and called out his wolf.

"Your eyes are gorgeous. Your teeth, fucking sexy." He took her mouth and ravished her. In and out he thrust into her. There was no holding back, no relishing in their lovemaking. His wolf was on a quest, a mission to fulfill this extra-special bond.

"Harder, Chordeo. Bite me now. Please," she stated through clenched teeth. He could hear her distressed voice through her fangs. It turned him on, making his cock grow plump and uncomfortable.

"Fuck!" he roared then exploded inside of her as he bit into her neck and she bit into his.

He felt himself lose focus as his blood left his veins and entered her mouth, her body, and her soul. It was outrageous and so surreal. *I love you. Together forever.* He heard her voice and felt himself relax. His wolf was content.

Opening his eyes, he squeezed her to him until he felt Chance tapping his arm.

One look at his brother's eyes and he knew he needed their mate now, too. "She is ours forever." He pulled slowly from Melena as she went willingly to Chance.

* * * *

Chance carried her over to the couch, sat down, and she straddled his waist.

He held her head and neck with his hand and stared up into her eyes. "You look amazing, mate. Your tousled hair, your plump breasts." He inhaled deeply, showing his own wolf teeth to her. "Your delicious scent."

She closed her eyes and he shook her hips. She lifted up and immediately took his cock into her pussy. Grabbing onto his shoulders, even her sharp nails that dug into his flesh turned Chance on.

"Harder, faster, mate. Ride me, so I can bite you, too."

Chance never felt so out of control. Melena had come to mean everything to him. Without her he would be nothing. He sensed Edric move in behind her and Chance lowered his body to give his brother room. There was no preamble as Melena reached back and grabbed a hold of Edric's cock.

"Now," she demanded with those damn sexy wolf-vampire fangs that made his cock release a bit of cum.

"I can't last," Chance admitted and began to thrust upward. Edric shoved into her ass from behind and Melena howled like a wolf. It wasn't loud or wild. It was low and sexual. Their wolves fed on that sensation and sound as Chance and Edric shoved into her. Chance exploded inside of Melena and she bit into his neck, sealing their fate. He growled low as content emotion filled his soul and calmed his wolf.

Edric continued to thrust into her, and then he exploded inside of her. Chance watched as Melena reached back, grabbed Edric by his hair, and pulled his face and neck over her shoulder. She bit into him as her breasts pushed forward. Chance cupped her breasts as he watched her teeth and mouth suck onto Edric and feed from his blood. His cock pulsated inside of her as he locked gazes with Edric.

His brother smiled and appeared in a drunken state.

"I'll never be the same again. I love you, Melena," Edric said. She smiled as Edric pulled from her ass.

Mano lifted Melena off of Chance and pulled her into his arms.

He hugged her to him as she straddled his waist. Chance chuckled as Mano looked around the room wondering where to make love to Melena.

Melena reached her hand down between them, used the muscles in her thighs to adjust her position and sank down onto his cock as Mano stood there.

* * * *

"Holy fuck," Mano said as Melena lifted up and down on his cock as he stood in the center of the room. He nearly lost his balance as she nipped along his neck and gripped his outer shoulders while fucking him hard. Taking a few steps forward, he reached the large mahogany desk and thrust on top of her. Pulling her thighs wider and grabbing her legs to wrap around him tightly, he stared down into her glowing, green eyes.

"Mine, now and forever." He stared at her swollen, large breasts, the blotchy love marks against her skin and her wet, sexy lips.

"Move, Mano, please, baby, I need it hard and fast." The sight of those fabulous teeth and the fact that she heard his thoughts and allowed him to see her own desires and need awed him.

"Holy fuck, you're going to bite me and feed from my blood. I want you so close to me. I want to brand you mine for eternity." He shoved into her harder, faster until he was so hard he exploded inside of her. She gripped his hair, pulled him closer, and bit into his neck. His cock pulsated inside of her cunt as his blood vacated his veins, entered her mouth and linked them like nothing he had ever imagined.

Mano licked across her neck, her breasts, then back to her mouth absorbing the feel of her in his arms.

"I love you, goddess."

"I love you, too."

Chapter 18

Melena looked out across land to the view from her family's estate in Honolulu, Hawaii. The warm tropical breeze caressed her skin as the evening began to fall upon them. The members of the Security Ring were set, the circle of elders secured, and precautions taken to ensure the safekeeping of the Book of the Founding Fathers. She knew exactly where it was and intended for it to remain there. Safe in the vault at Julius's home after the gods had directed her to its proper location. Morago left behind the diary of Dr. Henry Lesting which contained many disturbing experiments and ideas to destroy the Circle and were law. Her men feared that other copies of the book could be available, so it was now the work of the Secret Order to find those copies and destroy them. There was still so much work to be done.

In her heart, she felt content in knowing that her life would now be filled with pleasurable days with her wolves and nights with her vampire. She shed some tears for her family as she remembered the way they died and how she escaped from death. Her mates were there to support her and love her and she adored them for it. She closed her eyes as the sun began to set, a gorgeous orange, red, and yellow glow cast across the beach and she wished that Julius could enjoy it with her.

They were all bound together and now her true self, her ability to shift, and the powers of were, vampire, and magic flowed through her veins. Their love was powerful and always would be. In these moments, alone on the porch, the gods had revealed so much to her. She was filled with pride, despite the sadness that would surely take time to ease. Being on her family's land and facing her destiny with an open mind a healing heart made life worth living.

She took a deep breath, tilting her head up toward the brilliant sun.

It happened so fast. The reflection of sun against the blade of the knife as the man in black attempted to strike. She ducked from the first blow, then punched the man directly in the face. He countered, hitting her to the ground. In a flash he was dragging her from the house, pulling her between the trees by the deck.

Morago!

She cried out to her men as she continued to fight him.

Suddenly, something came over her. The hatred for this man and the fact that Morago killed her family and caused her such pain flowed through her veins. She felt the chills run through her body. He went to strike her again, but she somehow counter struck his blow.

"You've cost me everything. How did you not die with the rest of your stupid family?" he asked as he showed his wolf teeth and glared at her with hatred and disgust.

"How dare you step near this land, my land knowing that I would kill you?" she replied with just as much conviction.

"Ha!" He laughed at her as if she couldn't possibly have the ability or power to kill him.

Stupid wolf.

"My men should have killed you, too, back then. It's a mistake I'm here to rectify."

He bent for the knife and she moved toward it as well. Grabbing a hold of the knife she pointed it at him.

She could kill him right now. She could end all the feelings of hatred, loneliness, and despair by eliminating this awful, terrible wolf from existence.

"Stop!" Chordeo's voice echoed on the deck. He and the others were coming to her rescue.

She stared at Morago. The hatred in his eyes, her family's killer was right before her now. All those years she thought about what she would do when given the chance pervaded her mind.

"You deserve to die," she said as her teeth elongated and Morago's eyes turned to large saucers. As her men came running out as well as Vanderlan, she couldn't take her eyes off the target. All the killing, the massacre of her family and the hatred this wolf dispersed needed to be stopped. He couldn't remain free or alive. She sensed the need for revenge build up. In the last few days it had lessened. Her men helped her to see the importance of their bond and her position. But now that Morago just attempted to kill her, the need to kill him resurfaced. She could feel the evil trying to make her kill him.

"Kamea?" Gideon said her name.

She was nearly out of sorts. It was a struggle within herself. Kill Morago and rid this realm of his evildoing, or remember her position as a Goddess of the circle, not an enforcer of death. That was for the gods to handle, not her. What did it matter now that he was dead or alive? Her family was lost forever, but her survival would soon become even more important than anything she could ever want for herself. Revenge was temporary, once he was dead. Let the elders and the gods handle him.

She sensed her mates' approval of her thoughts. She felt their love, their ability to ease the hatred and shine light on the importance and power of their bond.

"Take him away. Let him suffer by answering to the gods and the circle of elders."

Vanderlan pulled Morago away from them and disappeared.

She tried to calm her breathing.

"Your eyes were glowing, and your teeth," Mano said in surprise.

She knew she had begun to shift. She was of the wolf completely. The magic of the gods had kept that a secret, even from Melena.

Big strong arms embraced her from behind and she gasped as Julius kissed the top of her head.

She turned into his hold.

"Julius! What are you doing? The sun," she stuttered, waiting for him to melt or cry out in pain but he didn't.

Instead he smiled at her then looked at the sunset.

"It is beautiful. I am glad to enjoy it with you."

The tears reached her eyes and as she stood on tiptoes to kiss him.

"Julius, how?" Edric asked. Mano and the others now surrounded Melena.

"Our mate has amazing powers. Her blood, mixed with mine, gives me the freedom to roam both day and night now."

"Then may I suggest you start working on your tan, buddy," Chance teased and they laughed.

Melena hugged Julius and reached her hand out to hold Gideon's. They all stood together on the deck and watched the sun disappear into the water.

"You're safe now, Kamea. No one can ever hurt you again," Gideon said.

"I'm home now. This is where I belong, and with the six of you by my side, we can ensure the protection and strength of were law for centuries to come. This is my home, my heritage. But I am afraid that I am far from safe, my mates. There is work to be done and spiritual creatures to protect. We can do it together."

In the distance the sounds of Polynesian drums performing the sunset dance echoed on the heels of the tropical breeze. She could hear her family, her ancestors' voices on the wind. As the Goddess of the circle, there would always be danger and always someone or something challenging the powers of the unknown. Kamea knew she was strong and determined to continue her family legacy and to do her part no matter what danger lay ahead. And there would be danger. She sensed it on the tip of the breeze that descended upon her as she stood with her men in paradise.

I will continue my father's legacy. I will protect the elders at all costs. Until the final three goddesses are located and secured in their position, the circle and were law will continue to be a target of our enemies. But for now, I will relish in being home, finding and loving my mates, and having peace of mind tonight that Morago is behind bars. One enemy down and only the gods know how many more to come.

Tilting her chin toward the warmth of the sun, she felt pride and peacefulness fill her soul. She was home again, the Polynesian, Goddess of the circle, the chosen one, and she would never feel alone again.

THE END

WWW.DIXIELYNNDWYER.COM

ABOUT THE AUTHOR

People seem to be more interested in my name than where I get my ideas for my stories from. So I might as well share the story behind my name with all my readers.

My momma was born and raised in New Orleans. At the age of twenty, she met and fell in love with an Irishman named Patrick Riley Dwyer. Needless to say, the family was a bit taken aback by this as they hoped she would marry a family friend. It was a modern day arranged marriage kind of thing and my momma downright refused.

Being that my momma's families were descendents of the original English speaking Southerners, they wanted the family blood line to stay pure. They were wealthy and my father's family was poor.

Despite attempts by my grandpapa to make Patrick leave and destroy the love between them, my parents married. They recently celebrated their sixtieth wedding anniversary.

I am one of six children born to Patrick and Lynn Dwyer. I am a combination of both Irish and a true Southern belle. With a name like Dixie Lynn Dwyer it's no wonder why people are curious about my name.

Just as my parents had a love story of their own, I grew up intrigued by the lifestyles of others. My imagination as well as my need to stray from the straight and narrow made me into the woman I am today.

For all titles by Dixie Lynn Dwyer, please visit
www.bookstrand.com/dixie-lynn-dwyer

Siren Publishing, Inc.
www.SirenPublishing.com

CPSIA information can be obtained at www.ICGtesting.com
Printed in the USA
BVOW11s2231270915

419821BV00010B/219/P